Echoes of the Past

Evan Bond

Published by Evan Bond, 2018.

This is a work of fiction. Similarities to real people, places, or events are entirely coincidental.

ECHOES OF THE PAST

First edition. December 31, 2018.

Written by Evan Bond.

Also by Evan Bond

Ethan McCormick Series
To the Wolves
Sins of the Mother

The After Death Series
After Death

Standalone
Death Can Wait
Getaway
Echoes of the Past
Charred Remains

Watch for more at https://www.evanbondauthor.com/.

To my wonderful editor and friend, Nicole.

Chapter One

I**t wasn't** the first time a knife had been held to her throat and it wouldn't be the last. The memory of her ex-husband crept up on her like a lion hunting its prey. She remembered the utter fear she had felt that night. Though she knew he wouldn't actually kill her, he was drunk enough to make a mistake. Sasha had known better to fight with him. Instead, she lay there and waited for his bout of anger to pass.

While she waited, she thought of her daughter Tara. If something awful happened, what would happen to Tara? Would he hurt her too? The thought of her daughter having to face the torment she did during his drinking fits scared her to death. It was the biggest fear of her life.

"Tara, sweetheart," Sasha started. "Are you comfortable back there?" Her daughter said she was fine but complained the trip was taking too long. Sasha smiled and shook the awful memories from her mind. "I know, honey, but we should be there very soon."

"But why are we moving so far away?"

"You know why, sweetheart."

"But I don't want to leave my life behind."

"Sometimes we need to do things we don't want to do. Sometimes we have to."

"Ok."

Tara stopped questioning her mother and continued playing on the tablet in her lap. Oblivious to her were the tears her mother now wiped away silently. Sasha felt like an awful mother. Making her move away from her school and all of her friends seemed like the worst thing to do to her. She was being uprooted from her life, from the only house she had ever known. All of her friends would become distant memories. It was upsetting for a girl of nine. Hell, it was upsetting for a woman of thirty-seven. But it was necessary. Sasha told herself she had to do it.

No one knew where they were going, not even Sasha's own mother. The abuse had become apparent to her in the end. In fact, it had been her idea for Sasha to leave. "Don't tell anyone where you're going," her mother had instructed. "It's best if we not know."

Sasha had taken her mother's advice and loaded a small trailer with anything that would fit. Taking Tara, they headed off to a small, New England town she could barely find on a map. They would be all but living off the grid like some sort of doomsday prepper family.

Up ahead stood a weathered sign with an overgrown tree hanging low enough to obscure it. The brown paint and yellow letters seemed faded and ignored. The beauty of the golden yellow and red leaves in the tree was lost on Sasha. Instead, she read the sign to herself. *Welcome to Carlisle, Maine. Est. 1692 Our Lands Whisper with the Echoes of the Past.*

The quote on the sign had been oddly beautiful. It was a poetic notion that only the early settlers of the country could have possibly written. She found herself inspired to learn as much about the town history as possible, once she was settled in of course.

Finding this small town had been a mere coincidence. When the plan to take Tara and run away had solidified in her mind, Sasha had called several real estate agents miles from her home. None could assist her due to the lack of funds. In fact, many had even laughed at her and hung up. Before she could feel defeated, however, she was given a tip to try a real estate company in Maine. Supposedly, their specialty was finding the right house for anyone on any budget. Naturally, Sasha had been skeptical but was left with no other choice.

The overly excited man nearly talked her ear all the way down to the floor. He would not shut up about the beautiful countryside and how gorgeous Maine was. Finally, he told her of a small house, which was more like a cottage, in a small town in Maine. Without much hesitation, Sasha had said she'd take it.

"Don't you want to see it first?" The man had asked. But it didn't much matter what it looked like. Sasha knew a Godsend when she saw one. This was her opportunity to leave her old life behind.

As the town rose into view, Sasha slipped a Xanax into her mouth and swallowed it dry. The thought of meeting everyone and explaining where she had come from, what little she could really share, did nothing for her stress levels. When she had told her psychiatrist about the move, she had prescribed extra medication, on top of the two pills she had to take daily for her depression. Psychiatrists really love their pills but they worked so Sasha didn't complain.

"Mommy, are we there?" Tara asked, placing the tablet in the seat next to her. Sasha nodded at her through the rearview mirror. She could see pure joy in her daughter's eyes. Not excitement for the new life she was being forced to create. Not for the joy of seeing their new home. No, her excitement was with ending her cramped existence in the backseat of the car.

Sasha pulled into the driveway and stared at her new home. It was small. Except, small wasn't the right word. The whole building could have fit inside a studio apartment. But what it lacked in indoor space it more than made up for with the yard. The backyard stretched for several yards before disappearing into the surrounding forest. A Thomas Kinkade painting came to mind as she stared at the cottage. Despite the size, it felt perfect.

Before Sasha could protest, Tara tore off down the driveway and into the cottage. Clearly, she was excited to get out of the car, stretch her legs, and probably pee. Sasha smiled and hoped there were other little girls in the town her daughter could get to know. She would desperately need a friend.

She spent the next couple of hours unloading the trailer. There wasn't much to unload and, lucky for her, the cottage had already been furnished. The furniture was old and rickety but it was all they needed. There wasn't a television anywhere in sight but she felt they could live without one for a while.

As she unpacked a box in the kitchen, a knock came at the door. Sasha knew it must be the inevitable neighbor greeting and put on her best fake smile. She pulled the door open and smiled at the seemingly cheerful woman on her doorstep.

"Hello there, you must be the new lady." Her New England accent was thick.

"That's me. My name's Sasha," she said, proffering her hand. The woman shook it and gave her a polite smile.

"Gwen," she responded. Spotting Tara on the couch, she said "Well, hello there little one. What's your name?"

"Tara," she said with a frown.

"What's wrong, dear?"

Tara shrugged and motioned to her tablet. "I can't get the internet to work."

Gwen laughed.

"We don't have a very good signal out here. It's best if you use a landline if you want to make phone calls or get online. It's tough on the young ones but that's how it is."

Sasha smiled. "I'll be sure to get that setup. Wouldn't want her getting bored out here. Not that there's much to be bored with," she nervously back peddled on her words, afraid she had offended the woman. "It's such a lovely town and the view is amazing."

"Yes, it really is. Well, I just wanted to welcome you to the neighborhood. If you ever need anything, I'm the next house down. It's a bit of a hike but a nice one. You two should come to the town center tomorrow evening and introduce yourselves. We're having a nice little fall festival."

"That sounds wonderful," Sasha said, though she wasn't sure if she meant it. Gwen smiled and said her good-byes. Seconds later, she and Tara were alone in their cozy little cottage once again. Things seemed to be going better than Sasha had expected. Her neighbors seemed friendly enough, at least the one she met. Not that it mattered to Sasha. Socializing was the farthest item on her list of things to do. Her depression made it hard to want to get out and make friends. Considering her situation, she wasn't overly willing to push through those feelings.

But she wondered if it would be good for Tara to get out and meet the people of the town. Maybe there would be some kids she could befriend. She would need them now more than ever. The choice was obvious but she still felt unsure. There were real benefits to getting her daughter out to socialize but it didn't matter. She couldn't quiet that voice in her mind that told her to bury her head in the sand. As always, she doubted and second-guessed her own decisions. If she went, she'd spend the whole time wondering if she had said the wrong thing or made herself look foolish. If she didn't go, she would become paranoid about what the town thought of her. Either way, she couldn't win. In the end, she had to think going was the better decision.

"Hey, Tara." She looked at her beautiful daughter sitting on the couch with a frown on her face. "You want to meet everyone tomorrow at a festival?" Tara shrugged. "It might be fun. You might meet a friend there. Maybe even a boyfriend."

Tara giggled. "Ew, I don't want a boyfriend."

Sasha smiled at her daughter's innocence, knowing one day it would vanish. She wasn't looking forward to those days and she prayed like hell she never developed the same disorder as her mother. Tara was too precious to suffer such debilitating thoughts. She deserved everything the world had to offer and should never experience pain like Sasha had endured through her life.

Emotions crashed over her like a rogue wave over the bow of a ship. She could feel herself sinking into the low pit of anguish and despair. The fight to suppress was nearly an impossible one. She knew she had to fight back the tears for the sake of her daughter, especially now. Tara finding her in a heap on the kitchen floor would do her no favors. Sasha managed to fight back her feelings and picked up an unpacked box. She headed into the bathroom with the excuse of unpacking.

Once the door was shut, she collapsed on the floor and everything flooded out of her at once. Her ex-husband, uprooting her daughter's life, the abuse, and her depression all flew through her mind at lightning speed. It played in her mind like a projector playing all her failures and mistakes back to her.

There was no stopping the memories now. The floodgates were open. A particularly nasty memory flashed through her mind and she winced as if in pain. Her husband had broken a beer bottle in the kitchen. The little pieces smashed against the wall and flew in every single direction. Beer dripped down the wall and formed a small puddle on the floor. She found her face crammed against the cold floor only inches from the puddle. She felt disgusting and pathetic as he had his way with her. All she could to not lose her mind was watch as the beer dripped down the wall until it was over. When he was finished, he told her to clean up the mess. Even now, she was unsure if he had meant the glass bottle and beer-stained wall or the disgusting substance his small member had left behind. Either way, she had done both.

Naturally, the memory only made her cry more. Even after leaving and getting far away from home, she couldn't stop feeling as if she had deserved it. After all, he would complain she didn't give it up enough and she always had some sort of excuse. He did the things he did because he was sexually frustrated. Rape was impossible, they were married. At least, that was what he had said when he found her in a bundle of depression on the bathroom floor the following morning.

"You know how I can get when I drink. Mix that together with sexual frustration and..." He had trailed off. Or maybe she had stopped listening. All she remembered now was that night had been the beginning of the end. For the first time ever, she had thought about hurting him, about fighting back. Multiple times he had threatened her with a knife, hammer, or whatever he had been holding at the moment. There would have been no question she had been defending herself.

Sasha sat up on the bathroom floor and wiped the tears from her face. The spiraling, it seemed, had come to an end. But these things always had a way of sneaking back up on her when she least suspected it. A tiny knock came at the door and Sasha jumped to her feet.

"Mommy, I have to pee."

"Alright, honey, just a second."

A brief glance in the mirror and Sasha touched up her hair and wiped away the smearing makeup. Sasha pulled open the bathroom door and smiled. "All yours," she said and headed off into the living room to unpack the remainder of the boxes.

Chapter Two

The **house** was completely silent, save for the cicadas outside with their endless chirping. Claire was used to them by now. In fact, they helped her sleep. She had lived in Carlisle for over thirty years and was used to the deafening silence inside her home and the utter roar of insects outside. It was a balance she had grown so accustomed to she couldn't sleep if it became disturbed.

An unfamiliar sound stirred her from her sleep. Though faint, the echo which muttered through her home was enough to disturb Claire. Somewhere off in the darkness of the house, something had been knocked off a counter. She was sure of it. But that was impossible. Claire lived alone and didn't own any animals. She wasn't the pet keeping type. She hated pets. They were disgusting creatures that provided nothing in return and only required handfuls of work. A truly pointless addition to a happy home, in her opinion.

Like most people, Claire's worst fear was an intruder. She was too old to protect herself in case someone wanted to do her harm. Though, there was no reason to fear. Her neighbors were all friendly and they all got along. Besides, no one in the history of Carlisle had ever committed a violent crime. Inside the city limits of Carlisle, there had never been a single murder. Three hundred years of peace and prosperity. Big city crimes just did not happen in Carlisle.

Even knowing the history of the town, she was still nervous. She couldn't explain why. Then the explanation hit her like a truck. A new woman had come to town today. No one in her thirty years in town had moved to Carlisle, and with good reason. There was nothing there. Modern Americans would feel like they stepped out of a time machine and into a less civilized world. There were no Wal-Marts for a hundred miles. No fast food restaurants, either. Sure, major updates had come to town over the years such as the internet, cable, modern plumbing, and electric cars. But, the structures remained relatively unchanged.

"Hello?" She called out into the darkness. Of course, there was no reply. She was being paranoid. It was an old house making noise, nothing more. She was merely on edge because of the newcomer. Tomorrow, at the fall festival, Claire would meet the woman and grow to love her. Then she would see there was nothing to worry about.

Still, she stared at the dark void that was the doorway to her bedroom. It had to be her eyes playing tricks on her but she could swear there were eyes staring back at her. Cold, glaring eyes seemed to pierce the darkness and into her soul. Nothing seemed to be attached. Merely eyes.

Claire shook her head and clamped her eyes. When she opened them, the vision was gone. She felt like she was going mad. Convinced she was seeing things, Claire rested her head back on the pillow and shut her eyes.

Somewhere in her bedroom, a floorboard creaked. Claire's eyes snapped open but it was too late. A gloved hand was placed over her mouth and held firmly. She tried to scream but it only came out in muffled whimpers. There was barely time for her to register what was happening before a large knife was driven straight through her skull. Her eyes rolled to the back of her head and urine soaked her pink nightgown. After a few twitches of the right foot, Claire was dead. The killer pulled the knife from her head with a sickening sucking noise and wiped the blood on either side of her cheeks, making the symbol of a cross. They weren't any ordinary crosses, however. These crosses were drawn upside down. A black candle the size of a small pickle jar was rolled under Claire's bed before the killer receded into the darkness.

Chapter Three

The morning air was crisp and clean. Sasha opened every window she could, letting in the morning sounds. For the first time in a long time, she was truly happy. It had to be the fresh air. Here, they were far from polluting cities and smog from car exhaust. Unlike the city she was used to, the air felt clean and fresh.

Tara was fast asleep in her bed. Considering the stressful situation Sasha had put her under, she decided to let her sleep in. Besides, a little alone time would be good for Sasha. As a single mother, she hardly had any time to herself.

There were still plenty of boxes to unpack but Sasha decided to brew herself a cup of coffee instead. While it brewed, she browsed over the furnishings in the cottage. Each piece looked more like it belonged in a museum than someone's home. But that didn't bother her. In fact, Sasha loved antiques. There was a certain excitement in never knowing what could be found while searching for antiques.

The coffee maker gurgled and made noise but had yet to dispense coffee. Sasha missed her Keurig. While she waited, she continued to explore the living room. The blue couch stood in the center of the room with a pink floral pattern draped across it. Wooden legs extended from the bottom and curled up like toes on the rug below. On either side of the couch stood an identical, rosewood end table. In several spots, especially on the drawers, there were chips of wood missing. Sasha thought it gave them character.

Sliding open one of the drawers, she found a bible tucked away. She shrugged it off and closed the drawer. Belief had never been a huge concern of hers. Too many terrible things happened around the world for her to accept a loving creator in the sky. Plus, her own life had been littered with misery and despair. She had heard a lot of people suffering from depression turned to faith. For her, it only pushed her farther away.

In the next drawer, she found a wax candle. The wick was slightly singed, signifying it had been lit perhaps once. She pulled it from the drawer and held it in her hands. It was the most peculiar candle she had ever seen. It was about the size of a mason jar and made entirely out of a solid piece of black wax. It hardly made any sense to stash a candle away in a drawer. What was the use of having a candle if it never got lit? Shrugging, she placed it on top of the end table and sat down on the couch.

If she were being honest with herself, she missed her television. There was nothing quite like sitting down in the early morning with a nice cup of coffee and a mindless talk show. Then, of course, at night it was always fun to binge watch her favorite Netflix show. Not having her TV would take some getting used to but she was certain she would. It might just take a while.

An aroma of coffee sprang through the home and Sasha stood up. As she poured herself a cup, she spotted a truck drive past the house. It was black with white doors and she was almost certain the words Carlisle Sheriff had been scrawled on the side. Judging by the dust cloud left in its wake, she assumed there was some sort of emergency. The notion nearly made her laugh. An emergency, out here? Did someone's chickens get loose? She could only assume the people out here had no clue what an emergency was. She, on the other hand, knew all too well.

It had been a rainy day, the first time she had called the police on her husband. She could recall the memory clearly, like most of the traumatic experiences in her life. Her husband, Brent, had been drinking. This time, like many times before, he had one too many. He was the kind of man who was fun to be around while drinking. As long as you didn't get him upset. Unfortunately, he was easily triggered when inebriated. And when you pissed him off while drunk, you might as well have tried to punch him in the face.

Tara, then only a six-year-old girl, was fast asleep in bed. Sasha wanted to keep it that way but Brent was having too much fun. He cranked the music on the disc player and started dancing around the living room like a buffoon. Sasha rolled her eyes and turned the music down.

"Tara's trying to sleep," she said.

"She'll be fine." Brent turned it back up.

Sasha wanted to unplug the damn thing and toss it out into the rain but remained silent. She tried to reason with him once more but he only shook his head and waved his butt in her face. When they were younger she would have found it funny, maybe even arousing. But all his years of drinking and verbal abuse had given her a disdain for him, though she was hard-pressed to admit it. Instead, she buried the emotion deep down inside herself like so many other emotions. She lied to herself, saying she still loved her husband. Tara needed them to stay together. Growing up in an unhappy marriage was better than a broken home. At least, that's what Sasha told herself.

Brent had sat on Sasha's knee and started singing along to the blaring music. He was only inches from her face and she could smell the disgusting scent of beer. He pretended to be a burlesque dancer and swayed on her knees, caressing her face with his hand. It annoyed her to her very core. "Please knock it off, you look ridiculous." She said and knew it had been a mistake before she had finished the sentence.

Instantly, his face turned an unnatural shade of red. To this day, she was almost convinced she saw smoke billow out of his ears like an old cartoon. His head vibrated with the telltale sign of gritted teeth. Sitting there on her knee, he raised a hand and slapped her hard across the face. The force had been enough to topple her to the floor, but her husband's weight across her lap kept her still.

She could feel the red mark left behind by his palm. It stung like a swarm of a thousand bees. Tears instinctively rolled down her face. Brent began to yell and scream in her face saying how much of a rude bitch she was.

"I'm trying to have fun with you and all you do is bitch. What the fuck is your problem you stupid whore?"

Sasha cried. "I'm sorry, it's just-"

She couldn't finish her sentence before he had grabbed a fistful of her hair and yanked her from her seat. The floor came up faster than she expected. Brent straddled her like a horse and bent down into her face. He screamed and yelled directly in her face. She could feel droplets of spittle splash on her cheek and the alcohol on his breath was revolting. Bile began to rise in her throat and she did her best to hold it down.

Sasha wiggled out from under Brent and ran down the hallway. As tears raced down her face, the television remote arced past her head and exploded against the wall. She dove into the bathroom and locked the door behind her.

He banged and pounded on the door, demanding she open it immediately. She sat down on the toilet, stuffed her face in her hands, and cried. Her biggest fear was Brent busting down the door to get to her. She would not have been surprised if he had.

"Go away or I'm calling the police" she screamed. It only worked to anger him more. He kicked the bathroom door and yelled the most obscene names she had ever heard. Finally, Sasha had had enough. She pulled out her cell phone and dialed.

The emergency operator quickly recognized the terror in her voice and helped calm her down. "Take a deep breath, explain the situation to me."

Sasha did her best to explain the night's events. Saying them aloud to another person made the event seem foolish. All this anger over something so simple. How could this really be happening? Now, she was afraid he would cause her bodily harm because of a simple request of silence and peace.

"Ma'am, where are you now?"

"I'm in the bathroom."

"Can he get in?"

"I don't think so."

"Ok, good. Just stay there. I have an officer on his way to your location now."

"What about my daughter? She's in her bedroom. What if he hurts her?"

"Is he mad at you or your daughter?"

"Me."

"Then he's not going to hurt her. The best thing you can do is stay where you are. An officer will be there shortly."

The operator had been correct. Less than five minutes later a patrol car had pulled into their driveway and the officer approached the front door. Sasha could hear Brent try to keep his composure as he answered the door and acted confused and surprised. From the bathroom, Sasha heard the officer call out for her. Quickly, she stepped out of the bathroom and approached the officer.

"Ma'am, are you OK?" He asked as she walked into the living room. She could feel his eyes fall on her cheek. Clearly, the mark was still visible. But Sasha remained silent and only nodded. With the police there, she felt foolish. Having them there was now only serving to embarrass her. She remembered wishing to take it all back. He would have calmed down on his own eventually.

“Mind if I talk to you outside for a moment, alone.” The cop looked at Brent after uttering the last word as if to accentuate his point. *Don't even try to follow us,* his tone said.

Sasha nodded and stepped past Brent nervously. There was a deep anger in his eyes. Of course, he had turned his head away from the officer to hide his glare. She would pay dearly for this later and she knew it. It had been a mistake. Once outside, the officer said, “Did he do that to you?”

“Yes, but it was an accident.”

“Ma’am, I’ve heard that excuse many times in my career. Never is it true. You can press charges, you know. We can take him in tonight and this can all be over.”

Sasha shook her head. "Can we just take him somewhere for the night? He'll be better tomorrow, I know it. He just needs to cool off."

The officer let out a sigh and watched Sasha intently. It was obvious he wanted her to press charges. She could almost feel him begging her to do so. But she couldn't bring herself to do it. To be honest, she was scared. Everything would change if he was hauled off to jail and that frightened her. Brent may have been a jackass, an alcoholic, and an abuser, but he provided. Sasha had not spent much time on her own and couldn't do much for herself. Without him, she would be lost. Somewhere in her subconscious, she knew Brent had molded her this way on purpose, though she would never admit it. Though, it didn't matter. He would get better one day. She had to believe he would. Things were tough right now, that was all. Money was tight. He was in line for a promotion at work. Once he got it, everything would improve.

"Are you sure? You really don't have to stand for this. We can process him and take care of all of this tonight."

Sasha shook her head again and tears rolled down her cheeks. "Please, just take him somewhere for the night. We'll be alright."

His eyes dropped and the corners of his mouth curled with disappointment. He stepped back inside and instructed Brent to gather whatever belongings he needed. "If you have a place you can stay, I'll take you there. You're going to sleep this off. Understand?"

Brent nodded but Sasha could tell he was already plotting. There was a familiar and sinister look in his eyes. She would obey his every command when he got home. She would have to. This was all her fault, or so she felt. If only she had not been so stupid and asked him to stop bothering her.

The coffee burned her tongue and she snapped back to the present. Her memory had been so vivid and lifelike. Now, she touched the spot on her cheek where he had slapped her. She could almost feel it. She remembered the terrifying and helpless feeling of being trapped in the bathroom while Brent slammed on the door. It was like something straight out of The Shining. Worst of all, she remembered the feeling of being to blame. She knew better now, though. No longer did she blame herself for the abuse. Brent had done it all to her and, in the end, he got what he deserved.

Chapter Four

"**You've got** to be kidding me," Sheriff Harrison said. He looked down at the small man who had reported the body inside Claire Shepard's home. Looking back up at the house, he shook his head.

"I couldn't believe it either. Claire's always outside watering her plants when I go for my morning run. I knew something was wrong when I didn't see her. Then I noticed the wide open door and..." he trailed off.

"Who the hell would do something like this? Claire Shepard never hurt a soul."

"I don't know Sheriff. It's awful. Nothing like this has ever happened here."

"Alright, Mason. Why don't you head home? I'll see what I can make of this. Oh, and don't tell anyone yet. Let me have a look around first. I'll call a town meeting later this afternoon."

"You got it, Sheriff," Mason said, visibly shaken.

Sheriff Harrison removed his hat and held it by his side as he entered the home. His boot heels clicked on the wooden floor as he made his way towards Claire's bedroom. There had never been a murder victim in Carlisle. He was not excited to see the first.

As he feared, it was a gruesome sight. Lying on the bed was the pale body of Claire Shepard, the woman who loved to bake cookies for her neighbors and always kept her garden fresh and lush. Reality had yet to set in for Sheriff Harrison. He was convinced he would wake up from this horrid nightmare any moment.

It took a few moments to gain composure. Eventually, Harrison worked up the courage to take a closer look at Claire's body. He expected the body to come to life and offer him a cup of tea. Claire Shepard had always been the inviting type. Staring at her lifeless corpse seemed unreal. The gaping wound in her head was definitive, though. There would be no coming back for this woman.

Cause of death had been a knife wound to the brain, that much was obvious. Blood had been streaked on her cheeks to resemble upside-down crosses. It was disturbing and confusing. Sheriff Harrison looked everywhere for a murder weapon but found nothing. All he found was a solid black candle under the bed.

He couldn't reach it with his arm so he hurried to the pantry and pulled Claire's broom free. Back in her room, he lay on the floor and scooped it towards him. There was nothing particularly special about the candle other than the fact it was solid black. The wick was barely used. Harrison knew it didn't belong to Claire. The old woman had always criticized others for keeping candles in the house. "You're asking for a house fire," she used to always say. His instincts told him the candle was important but he couldn't see how.

Realizing he should dust it for prints, he placed it down on the floor and hoped he hadn't ruined his chances of finding the killer. He remained confident if there were prints from the killer, he'd find them. Of course, that was assuming the killer had not worn gloves.

There had never been a single murder in Carlisle since Harrison had become Sheriff. He was certain there hadn't been any before that either. Sure, there had been some drunken bar fights, some unruly people, but nothing an overnight visit in a jail cell couldn't fix. But murder? That was something wildly different. It was something Harrison had seen only in television shows and preferred it that way. Once word spread that Claire Shepard had been murdered, the whole town would be swept into a frenzy. He had to be delicate about the situation. There was no telling how the townspeople would react. Hell, *he* didn't even know how to react yet.

He went about inspecting the body and everything in the bedroom. Nothing seemed to be out of place or missing. Robbery was ruled out. A revenge killing was unlikely, as no one had problems with Claire. She had no relatives in town and hardly had any money, so financial gain was, doubtfully, the motive. Whichever way Harrison looked at it, he could think of no reason why someone would want Claire dead.

Sheriff Harrison shook his head in confusion. The only motive which seemed to make any sense was one he was utterly terrified of. Someone in town had snapped. They had to be dealing with a psychopath, it was the only explanation.

He walked back to his truck and picked up the radio receiver off the passenger seat. Calling it in, he requested the local morgue send a van out for the body right away. The deputy was also called to the scene to help catalogue and take pictures. They were going to have a lot of work ahead of them.

Chapter Five

Her morning was spent organizing things into their proper places and folding up cardboard boxes. Tara played in the backyard while her mother worked to finish unpacking. Sasha envied her daughter. In spite of this dismal and dark life, she was able to play and enjoy life. Sasha, on the other hand, had a hard time seeing the silver lining even in the best of times. She could only hope her daughter didn't develop the same disorder as her. Sasha wanted Tara to do whatever she wanted in life. There could be nothing holding her back. This depression would do nothing but. It was an awful disorder that pulled her away from so many wonderful things. Tara didn't deserve it. Sasha knew in her heart her daughter was meant for great things. But what parent didn't think that of their child?

The town would be having a festival later that night and Sasha felt torn. It would be a good idea to meet the townspeople and mingle a bit but she really didn't want to. Most people she knew never understood her reluctance to socialize. Some thought she was being dramatic. Others thought she was looking for attention. The truth was, a lot of social events gave her uncontrollable anxiety. Merely thinking about being in a room full of strangers made her chest hurt. It was a feeling she had lived with for quite some time and yet was still not used to.

The house was beginning to feel cold and dark. Sasha snatched up the candle and looked for a box of matches. She lit the candle and placed it in the center of the kitchen table. Staring at the flame as it danced in the subtle air flow seemed to ease her mind. Something about fire had always calmed her down. The mesmerizing flicker always sent her into a sort of hypnotic state.

She realized she could no longer hear Tara playing outside. She probably had tired herself out but Sasha decided to check on her anyway. There was nothing but an empty field and the forest behind the house. Sasha's heart thudded against her sternum.

She slipped on her shoes and dashed out the back door, calling her daughter's name. Her voice echoed back at her through the trees. When Tara didn't respond, she began to panic. She stared at the dense woods and wondered if Tara had wandered inside.

Without a second thought, she bolted across the yard and into the trees. She called out her daughter's name and tried to calm her shaking hands. This couldn't be happening. She couldn't lose her daughter. It would be too much for her to handle. There had to be a simple solution to the matter. Tara had merely wandered off to explore the woods. Nothing sinister. She hoped to God it was true.

"Mommy?" A small voice echoed.

"Yes, sweetheart. Where are you?"

"Over here."

Tara did not sound distressed but it did nothing to calm Sasha's nerves. There would be no calm for her until her daughter was securely in her arms. She ran in the direction of the echoing voice and finally found her daughter. Tara stood in the center of a small clearing with an object in her hand. Barely noticing the object, Sasha ran to her daughter's side and wrapped her arms around her.

"Mommy," she said, pulling away. "Look what I found. Isn't it cool?"

Sasha looked at her hand and spotted a peculiar knife. It looked like it was made of bone.

"Don't touch that" Sasha said, snatching the knife from her daughter's hand and tossing it back on the ground. "Come on, we're going back home. Don't ever run off into the woods like that again. I thought something terrible happened to you."

"But mom-"

"Don't talk back to me. Do as I say, understand?"

Tara nodded and they made the trek back to the house. Slowly, Sasha's heart began to return to a normal pace. Her daughter had scared the living daylights out of her. She did her best not to seem mad at her. The last thing she wanted to do was push her daughter away but she had to understand the rules. She couldn't just wander off like that, especially in an unfamiliar town.

When they got home, Tara ran off into her bedroom and closed the door. Clearly, she was mad at her mother for ruining her day of fun. Sasha felt terrible but stood firm. Tara couldn't run off like that until they knew this town better. Who knew what kind of people lived here? Maybe not now, but one day Tara would understand.

• • • •

ACROSS TOWN, a small gathering of neighbors met inside a living room furnished with items from eras long past. This group met once a week, always meeting in the same home with the old furniture and dust covered seats. There wasn't much in the town of Carlisle and for these four individuals, gossip was all they had. Mostly they spoke of trivial things like which yards could use a good mowing and who was stealing newspapers off Old Man Brady's porch. It was a kid, no doubt about that. Probably some bored child whose parents were not doing a good job of watching but it was more fun to pretend it was something sinister.

Today, however, was different. Something had *actually* happened in Carlisle. Something that had not happened in a long time. The group had gathered as quickly as possible to discuss the news. Not the body found earlier this morning. They had yet to hear about it. Instead, they gathered in the old woman's living room to discuss the appearance of a new member to their community. It had set the town ablaze with rumor. Everyone wanted to know her every detail. Where had she lived before? Why did she leave? And just what the hell was she doing out here in the middle of nowhere?

“I hear she's from a big city. City people don't end up out here unless they're running from something.” Josh Gruber said.

“Or someone” Betty Myer finished.

“I heard her husband sexually molested her daughter and they both ran away.” Kyle Ferguson said. The rest of the group groaned. Kyle couldn't help but mention the most disgusting explanations. Half the time, he had simply made them up. Josh always thought he would make for a great shock jock out in the city.

“Where'd you hear that, Kyle?” Betty asked.

“Sheriff Harrison mentioned it to John Williams and he told Brian who told me.”

“A friend of a friend, huh?” Josh asked. Everyone, except for Kyle, laughed.

"I heard she finished with a nasty divorce and was looking to get away from it all. Her ex-husband was the drinking and beating type, you know?" Carol Leighter said. She was always the sensible one and was usually right in her gossip. When Carol spoke, it usually came from a place of knowing.

"See, I could still be right. Guys like that can always do terrible things." Kyle insisted.

"Oh please, Kyle. No one wants to hear that." Carol said.

"No one ever wants to hear it."

Carol rolled her eyes and the group collectively groaned. They continued with their gossip of Sasha and her daughter Tara, going with Carol's abusive husband theory. After all, it was the most sensible. Moving to Carlisle proved she was hiding from something. So, the theory fit right in.

The gossip continued, more coffee was consumed, and ideas shared. A knock at the front door brought a silence over the group. They weren't used to visitors during their sessions. Everyone in town knew to leave them alone when they gathered. Otherwise, they could fall prey to a false rumor in retaliation. Nothing horrible, just little rumors like so-and-so forgets to wear deodorant or has a secret obsession with dirty magazines. It got people talking but not enough to ruin lives.

Betty answered the door and was greeted by Sheriff Harrison. She smiled and gave him a wave.

"Morning, Betty." He said.

"Morning, Sheriff. What can I do for you?"

Sheriff Harrison rolled his shoulders and cleared his throat.

"Well, I was hoping you could spread the word about a town hall meeting this afternoon at the community center."

"I suppose. What's it about?"

"You'll find out at the meeting. Please, let everyone know, OK?"

Betty nodded and watched as the sheriff walked away and drove off in his truck. Turning around to face the others, they began to gossip harder than before. Something was up in the small town of Carlisle. And they were certain the new girl in town had something to do with it.

• • • •

SASHA HAD finally finished unpacking the last of her boxes when someone knocked on the front door. She figured it was another friendly neighbor coming by to welcome her to the neighborhood. Putting on a fake smile, she prepared to be courteous and friendly. She opened the door, ready to greet the well-meaning neighbor and stopped in her tracks. A man dressed in khaki pants, brown collared shirt, and a sheriff hat stood outside her door. His gold badge sparkled in the morning sun.

"Ma'am, I'm Sheriff David Harrison. First of all, welcome to our little town." He proffered his hand and Sasha took it.

"My name's Sasha. My daughter Tara is sulking in her room right now. It's nice to meet you, Sheriff Harrison."

"I wanted to let you know, personally, since you're new to town and might not hear otherwise, there's a town hall meeting this afternoon at the community center. We're hoping everyone will attend. There's an announcement I need to make."

"Oh? I hope it isn't bad news."

"I'm afraid it is. Hope to see you there. You know where the community center is?"

Sasha nodded, though she wasn't entirely sure. She was sure, however, she could figure it out. Sheriff Harrison gave her a nod and spun towards his truck. Sasha watched him as he walked away. He was a handsome man with a kind and caring face. His toned body wasn't bad either. She thought about asking him to show her around town but thought better of it. Besides, her depression had kicked in hard. Her mind scolded her for thinking she could truly be happy or find someone who would actually like her. She was a mess and would always be a mess. No man would want her. Surely not a kind, caring, and attractive man such as Sheriff Harrison. And if someone like him did, well, they would turn out to be just like Brent. Their kind and caring nature was merely a show for the woman they intended to capture. Once locked in, all bets were off. Their true nature would bubble to the surface like magma through a volcano. Their anger and hatred and rage would show itself. Then, she would be right back with *him*. The monster she had worked so hard to get away from would be back in her life, only with a new mask. The mask of a nice-looking man who worked as Sheriff in a small town. Sasha wiped the tears from her face and did her best to quiet her brain.

She looked at the clock in the dining room and saw it was only a few minutes past ten in the morning. There was plenty of time before the town hall meeting. It would take her a while to gain enough composure to go out in public. It was bad enough for her to mingle with people she knew. But strangers? That would almost be impossible. Maybe, she could stick close to Sheriff Harrison. He could make her feel safe. The familiar and menacing tone of her own thoughts returned to tell her it would never work. Sasha shook her head to clear the thoughts and went back about her business.

Chapter Six

The **community** center stood in the center of town. It was a large building which easily fit the miniscule population of Carlisle inside and yet it still felt cramped. Now, people gathered eagerly inside waiting for whatever news the Sheriff had to share. To Sasha, it felt like thousands of people had crammed their way inside. Had the town population doubled in size in the last few hours? She knew looks could be deceptive, though. Sasha knew that better than most people.

All the important buildings of Carlisle were lumped into one small grouping in the center of town. The community center sat between city hall and the sheriff's office. A few yards away stood the library. The schoolhouse could be seen from the community center front window, though it was across the street. A few shops made up the other areas of the city center and Sasha made a mental note to explore a few of them. That was if she ever felt strong enough to get out of the house.

Many of the citizens of Carlisle walked by Sasha. Some greeted her with a friendly wave, others introduced themselves with a handshake, and several turned their noses up at her. She did her best to ignore these people but it was rather difficult. Hadn't these people been taught any manners? What had she done to deserve it? People sometimes despised change, she understood that. But, most people faked a smile and pretended to be polite. These individuals wanted her to know how they felt. Maybe it was their way of attempting to run her out of town. Well, they were in for a disappointment because she was stuck there for the time being. There was nowhere else for her to go.

Everyone took their seats as Sheriff Harrison stepped into the building and headed for the stage. Sasha hoped the meeting wouldn't take long. The wooden chairs built into the community hall were uncomfortable.

"I'm going to cut right to the chase," Sheriff Harrison boomed into the mic as he removed his hat. "This morning, Claire Shepard passed away."

The crowd murmured quietly. Sasha was confused. Why would they call a meeting about some, presumably, old lady dying in her sleep? That couldn't possibly have been big news around here. Unless she hadn't just been some old lady who died in her sleep. Maybe she was a founding member of the town? But that couldn't be right. Hadn't the sign on the drive in said founded in the 1600's? She was sure it had. Perhaps this Claire woman was important to the town in other ways, like a mayor's wife or something like that. Maybe, she was the first person to ever die in Carlisle. Sasha's imagination ran wild. She pictured a town full of immortal beings. They looked like regular people, talked like regular people, except they didn't die like regular people. Then, one day, one of them did die. Was that what was happening here? Hadn't she taken a wrong turn on the highway and found herself smack in the middle of a Stephen King novel?

"I can't discuss all of the details at this time because it is an ongoing investigation. However, we are suspecting foul play. It appears Ms. Shepard was murdered in her bed-" A thunderous roar of voices drowned out Sheriff Harrison completely. His attempts to regain control of the crowd were fruitless. Sasha cupped her hands over Tara's ears to keep them safe from the screaming mob.

They were scared, that much was obvious. Sasha understood. This was a small town. Everyone knew everybody. A murderer among them must have been similar to finding out your brother was a killer. It was a scary thought to think one person among so few could be a killer.

"Is there a suspect?" A voice cried out from the crowd.

Before Harrison could answer, another voice said, "What type of weapon did they use?"

"Are we all in danger?"

"Who could do such a thing?"

The questions began to melt together as everyone began talking over each other. Sheriff Harrison yelled at the top of his lungs from on stage but no one seemed to pay any attention. The crowd was whipped up into a violent frenzy.

Sasha could see the struggle on Sheriff Harrison's face. He needed to get control of the crowd and quick. Fear turned people into chaotic and terrifying creatures. Harrison reached for his sidearm and fired one shot into the air. The whole room stopped and stared at him in surprise.

"Everyone, please take your seats and try to remain calm. We don't have all of the answers yet but I promise I'll keep you informed every step of the way. Whoever is responsible for Claire Shepards' death will pay to the full extent of the law. You have my word on this. But we can't start panicking now. I need your help. You need to stay calm and report anything out of the ordinary, anything suspicious. Nothing is too small. Bring it to my attention and I'll look into it. We're going to get to the bottom of this case, everyone. Until then, stay safe and know that I'm doing everything I can to bring this person to justice."

His speech seemed to ease the town into a forced state of calm. Clearly, they were all still nervous but the faith they had in sheriff Harrison was astounding. They were able to look past their fear and follow him into whatever darkness their future held. It was an arousing quality. Sasha found herself daydreaming about going out to dinner with the man. The familiar voice of inadequacy reared its ugly head.

"On a more positive note," Sheriff Harrison stated. "I would like to officially welcome the newest member of our little community of Carlisle. Ms. Sasha Jameson and her daughter Tara. Please, stand up and give a wave." Reluctantly, Sasha did just that. She smiled at the sea of faces staring back at her. More than anything, she wanted to run out of that room and hide under her blankets.

"I want everyone to take time out of their day to make her feel welcome. She's new to our community. Let's show her what a nice one it is, OK?" The crowd gave a half-hearted applause and Sasha sat back in her seat, her face growing hot and red.

When the town meeting was over, Sasha led Tara back towards home. They stopped a few times as neighbors introduced themselves and welcomed them. It was a nice gesture but she wanted to get back home to the safety of being alone. She smiled, nodded, and walked past several people who said hello. She felt like the rudest person in the world but her anxiety was reaching max levels. Hearing about the murder and being put on the spot by the Sheriff immediately after had really done a number on her nerves. This had been the worst day to leave the bottle of Xanax in the medicine cabinet.

The moment she was home, she swallowed one down without water and flopped on her bed. Tara went back to playing in her room without a care in the world. Sasha felt so much envy for the naivety of her daughter. If Tara were lucky, she'd never inherit Sasha's problem. Her eyelids began to grow heavy and she let her head fall against the pillow. In a matter of seconds, she was fast asleep.

When she finally woke up it was dark outside. Groggy and confused, she headed to the kitchen for a glass of water. The Xanax really helped her anxiety but she hated the way it made her feel. Zombie-like was the best way she could describe it.

The room temperature water did wonders for her dry mouth and she leaned against the sink in relief. Sasha looked over at the clock. It was seven in the evening. She felt guilty for leaving Tara alone for so long. *She's being awfully quiet*, Sasha thought. It may have merely been the talk of murder but she felt on edge. If fear were a monster it could be found digging its claws into Sasha's skull and planting itself in her brain.

She ran from the living room, dropping the glass on the floor. It shattered off in the distance but her brain was too preoccupied to hear it. Terrible images of death and horror flashed through her mind. She fought back tears as she turned the corner and into Tara's room. Lying there in the middle of the bed, face down, was her daughter. She had fallen fast asleep. Sasha let out a sigh of relief and slowly approached her daughter's bed.

Pulling the covers up over Tara, Sasha gave her a kiss on the head and walked out of the room. Relieved that nothing was wrong, Sasha made her way back to the kitchen and began to sweep up the glass.

• • • •

THE CLEARING in the woods behind Sasha's home was not empty. A masked man dragged an elderly woman by the hair through the dirt and fallen leaves. A thick piece of duct tape had been secured over her mouth and her wrists were bound by ropes. Her eyes were red and puffy from where she had been crying. A small stream of blood trickled from her eyebrow from where the man had struck her.

Even now, she cried and mumbled through the tape, begging her captor to let her go. He barely recognized her cries for help. To her, he didn't even seem human. He dropped her in the center of the clearing and began to search around. While his back was turned, the woman began to slither away like a wounded snake from a hawk. Before she could get far, she felt his hand wrap around her left ankle and yank her back.

Before she could react, she was spun onto her back and straddled by the masked man. In his right hand, he held a white knife which looked to be made of bone. She cried harder than she had ever done in her life. Urine streamed down her leg as the man brought the knife down on her chest. She felt the white-hot pain before she heard her sternum crack. Blood poured from the wound and soaked the dirt beneath her body.

A pain, unlike any pain she had ever felt before, erupted through her body. In an effort of survival, she desperately tried to flail her arms and legs. Terror gripped her as she realized she could no longer feel them. Her body felt cold and numb now. Her attacker stood over her with the bone knife clutched in his hand, her blood still dripping from the blade. His gloved hand was gripped tightly around the handle. Darkness seeped into her vision and she could feel herself slipping away. The last thing she saw before her world went dark was her attacker removing his mask and smiling down at her. It was a crooked and evil smile from a strange man she had never seen. In her final moment of life, she truly thought the devil had come to collect her soul.

Chapter Seven

Sheriff Harrison was a tough man. He had served in the gulf war, winning several medals. Some of the horrific sights still kept him up at night. The bodies of friends, innocent civilians, and enemies crowded his memories. Before him now was one of the most horrendous sights he had ever seen. Eileen Granger, an elderly woman who mostly kept to herself, had been stripped naked and left in the woods. Her chest hung open like a zippered tote bag, the bits of jagged skin substituting for the zipper. It was hard to tell at first glance because of the amount of blood and carnage but her heart was missing. Harrison would have suspected wolves had it not been for the bone knife resting only a few feet away from the body. Somehow, a person had managed this. It seemed almost inhuman.

Harrison swallowed hard, not wanting to vomit in the crime scene. The gray tape over Ms. Granger's mouth was stained with blood. Her eyes were frozen open in a look of sheer horror. Worst of all, they bulged out of her head farther than he thought humanly possible. Much like the body of Ms. Shepard, upside down crosses had been drawn on her cheeks with her own blood. Harrison didn't want to admit it even to himself. There was a serial killer in Carlisle.

But why? Of course, that was always the question when someone took a life. A more important question, at least to Harrison, was who was next? Sheriff Harrison intended to find the killer before more people turned up dead. He would have to. A second victim would whip the town into a panic. There'd be no controlling the storm. Even in big cities, fear gripped the communities affected by murder. He could only imagine the fear a small town like Carlisle would handle it. Especially one which had never dealt with it before.

For only a moment, Sheriff Harrison thought about sweeping the whole thing under the rug. Perhaps he would tell the town she had been attacked by a bear or a wolf. He dismissed the thought. They needed someone to trust in right now. If they were to learn the sheriff, the one person sworn to keep them all safe had lied...well, there'd be no town left to protect.

With a gloved hand, he picked up the nearby knife. The white blade and handle were stained with crimson splotches. Harrison thought it looked more like a piece of bone than a knife. It must have been carved from the rib of some sort of animal. At least, he hoped it had been an animal. He shuddered and slipped it into an evidence bag. After, he took a few pictures with the camera on his phone, forwarded them to his work email, and called the mortuary. He would want them to be ready for an autopsy.

While he waited for the body to be picked up, Harrison had a look around. There were obvious drag marks in the dirt leading to the clearing. A huge area of dirt had been disturbed, suggesting she struggled to get free. He truly wished she had been able to wiggle free. He wanted it all to stop. Things like this never happened here. It was the whole reason he chose to be a small town sheriff. There was no excitement, no car chases, no dead bodies, no drug dealers. Nothing. Carlisle had been the perfect town, until now.

The body had not been the most disturbing part of this particular murder. No, that came in the form of an unusual letter in Harrison's mailbox this morning. When he had gone outside to retrieve the local paper, as he did every morning, he noticed the little red flag on the mailbox was up. He knew there was nothing he had been trying to mail so he chalked it up to young kids playing pranks in the night. Harmless fun. Harrison himself had partaken in similar acts as a teenager. Curious, he pulled open the mailbox anyway. He found a folded-up slip of paper inside.

He grabbed it and unfolded the edges carefully, not sure what to expect. The note was handwritten and somewhat sloppy. Either a man with a heavy hand a quick writing style or someone writing in the dark. The note explained the exact location of a body in the woods. The directions were clear and concise. There was no doubt the killer had left the note, not some anonymous tipper. Thinking about the killer standing in front of his yard, touching his mailbox, gave him chills. He couldn't believe it. This couldn't be real. It was something ripped straight from one of the detective novels he read quietly on his back porch.

Harrison now stared at the wrinkled and bloodstained body before him. It was all too real. No childish pranks. This killer was the real deal. It was an awful truth plaguing this town. His next move would not be an easy one. "Jesus," he said to himself. "How do I break the news this time?"

Chapter Eight

The morning was crisp and beautiful. Birds chirped in the trees, morning dew dripped from vibrant blades of green grass, and a cool breeze blew in from the north. All of this, however, was lost on Sasha. Her depression and anxiety had flared up to levels of intensity once again. It wasn't always easy to figure out where these mood swings came from. Often, there was no answer and she was forced to ride them out like some sort of horrible amusement park ride. Of course, it didn't mean she could ignore her motherly duties. Sasha couldn't afford to take a break. Being an only parent with crippling depression was difficult, to say the least.

"Good morning, sweetheart." Sasha greeted her messy haired daughter who sat slouched at the kitchen table. "How did you sleep?"

"Good I guess."

Sasha smiled.

"Glad to hear it, sweetie. I'm making pancakes if you want some."

"Yes."

"Yes, what?"

"Yes, please."

Sasha smiled again. Even when her mind was at its worst, Tara always found a way to make her smile with no effort at all. Sasha was certain her daughter was a peace offering from God. A benefaction for the life she had been forced to live.

Sasha brought the plate of freshly made pancakes over to the table and set them down gently. Tara began to dig in without a second thought. Sasha smiled and returned to the kitchen to refill her empty coffee cup.

"Mommy," she heard Tara call from the dining room. "Are you not going to eat any?"

Sasha shook her head. Looking at her daughter from the small pass-through between the two rooms she said, "Mommy's not hungry" She gulped down the lie with a swig of lukewarm coffee. If she had been honest with her daughter, she would have told her she was, in fact, hungry but her stomach was tangled in painful knots. She wouldn't be able to keep food down if she tried. Maybe later when everything had finally settled down she would get something in her belly. If she had known about the mutilated corpse Sheriff Harrison had found only a few yards from her home, she might have never eaten again. At least, not without picturing such a grotesque scene.

When Tara finished eating, she ran off to her bedroom to change. Within seconds, she was heading for the back door. "Hold on. Where are you going?"

"Outside. The leaves are pretty and I want to play in them."

"I don't know. The last time you went outside-"

"I won't run off, mom. I promise."

"You'll stay where I can see you?"

"Yes."

"You promise?"

"I swear."

Sasha nodded reluctantly and watched as Tara cheered and opened the door. More than anything, Sasha wanted to join her daughter but her nerves were far too shot. Instead, she would sit on the couch and attempt to calm herself down. The little orange bottle of Xanax danced in her mind, taunting her to take one. She would hold out as long as she could, hating the way they made her feel.

She closed her eyes and tried some of the calming techniques her therapist had taught her. She was only part way through picturing herself on a tranquil beach when she heard a scream that turned her blood to ice. Before Sasha could even register what was happening, she was up from the couch and running out the door. Instincts took over and she snatched her daughter from the ground. Tara pointed down at the grass near the base of the home and Sasha knew instantly what had scared her. A human heart, still dripping with fresh blood, rested only a few feet away.

Bile rose in her throat as she rushed her daughter inside, forcing herself to choke it back down. Sasha called the police and a deputy told her the sheriff was on call and would be there as soon as he could. Sasha did her best to thank the unconcerned sounding man and hung up.

Less than five minutes later, the sheriff was knocking at the door. Sasha was relieved with his response time but also a little shocked. She swung open the door with a grunt of panic and stared at the man at her front door. "That was quick." She said.

"I was in the neighborhood."

Sasha scanned the driveway and noticed his truck was missing.

"How did you get here?"

"I was very close. Please, may I come in?"

Sasha ushered the sheriff into her home and offered him some coffee, to which he politely declined. She nodded and tried to hide the fact she was shaking, though she knew she was doing a poor job.

"Smith tells me you found something in your backyard."

"My daughter did, actually."

"Sorry about that."

Sasha nodded.

"What did she find?"

"It's better if I just show you, I think."

Sasha led Harrison to the backyard and pointed at the heart still sitting there. Harrison coughed, clearly not expecting to see it.

"Jesus Christ," he said.

"Yeah, how do I explain this to my daughter?" Sasha asked, averting her eyes from the bloody organ. "Better question, why is there a heart on my lawn?" She was close to screaming now. "Is it some sort of terrible prank because we're new? Is this how the town tells us we're not welcome?"

"Of course, not-"

"Then are me and my daughter in danger?"

"Please, allow me to exp-"

"You're the sheriff, you need to do something about this. First the dead woman and now there are organs showing up on my lawn. What kind of shit is this place into?"

"Ma'am, please calm down and I'll explain everything to you."

Sasha placed her hands against her temples, nursing a major headache. The stress was too much to handle. She needed that Xanax now but she refused to take it. Sheriff Harrison took her by the hand and ushered her inside. Getting her a glass of water, he sat her on the couch and did his best to relax her.

"Here's the thing, and please keep this between us for now. There was another body found."

"What?"

"Yes, this morning in fact. The scene was morbid. The victim's heart was missing."

"Oh my God."

"I have no idea why it was left at your house. It may have been dropped by mistake."

"How could it have been dropped by mistake at my house?"

"Well, the body was found in a small clearing in the woods not too far from here."

Sasha's blood ran cold. She knew the very spot. Tara had found it only yesterday. Her hands began to shake in terror. Was the killer out there when she had fetched Tara from the woods? Was he watching them? Could Tara have been killed if she had not made it to her in time? Maybe the heart was a warning they were next. Her mind raced with idea after idea until she could no longer take it. Out of breath, she raced into the kitchen and grabbed the little orange bottle, spilling several pills on the counter. Harrison watched as she gulped down a pill and nearly vomited in the sink.

When the panic attack began to subside, she started to feel ashamed. She couldn't help it. It was embarrassing. It was beyond embarrassing.

"I'm so sorry about that."

"Please, don't be. I understand."

"Do you? Do you understand what it's like to lose sleep because you can't shut off your mind? Do you understand what it's like to hate yourself and spend every waking moment scared of what might go wrong? Or, do you understand what it's like to believe that your family would live a better life without you?"

Sasha breathed heavily now, regretting everything she had said. It had been nothing more than an angry outburst. At least, it's what she wanted to believe. But something happened that she had not expected. Sheriff Harrison looked up at her with a single tear rolling down his cheek.

"In fact, I do. I served during the Gulf War. Two tours, actually. I went over there thinking I was protecting freedom, my country, and my family. But, I came back different. I would sit in my bedroom in complete darkness for days and wouldn't even speak to my family. I would contemplate signing up for a third tour, only to let some towel head off me to save my family the torture of watching me whither away to nothing. I lost my family because I wasn't the same person. I understand all too well what it's like to hate yourself."

Sasha sat down next to Harrison and placed a hand on his shoulder. There were no words she could have said at that moment to make him feel better. People always felt the need to say something but sometimes it was better to just be there. Sasha understood that. It felt good knowing someone who could relate to her. Finally, she didn't feel so alone in this world.

"I'm sorry, ma'am, I should get your yard cleaned up for you. I'll have my deputy out here right away to take care of it. If you need anything," he wrote down a number on the back of a slip of paper. "Call me directly, alright?" Sasha nodded as she took the paper from his hand, their fingers briefly touching.

Before Harrison walked out the front door, he stopped and looked at something in her living room. Sasha followed his gaze to the black candle she had found in the end table. She thought there was a look of suspicion in his eyes before turning back to guilt. He then headed out the door.

As promised, the deputy arrived and the heart was bagged into evidence. The deputy was nice enough but seemed a little socially awkward, though Sasha couldn't judge. She knew she was as socially awkward as they come. He gave her a smile and a wave as he jumped back in his truck and headed back to the station.

Sasha was left wondering about the, now, double homicide plaguing the town and why part of the body had been left in her yard. It couldn't have been a coincidence. There had to be a meaning behind it, but what? Her mind raced with the possibilities until she felt herself become too drowsy to think. Knowing she couldn't sleep, she got up on her feet and began to work on any chores she could think of.

Her mind slipped to a place where she did not want to be. Memories of her ex-husband were the last thing she wanted on her mind. But they flooded back all the same. Attending to random chores had always been a good way for her to avoid contact with her ex-husband. She had avoided many violent outbursts and sexually charged beatings by doing something useful around the house. He hated lifting a finger so much he would avoid her while she was working, even if he was furious with her. Her only defense had been to work long enough until he had passed out from drinking. Only then had she been able to relax. Though, it did not always produce the result she had wanted.

One night, in particular, she had taken up organizing the kitchen drawers. She claimed they were getting far too cluttered and needed to be adjusted. Brent had been out drinking at a local bar, one of his usual hangouts. When he came home, he was ready to have his way with his wife. Sasha, not wanting to be degraded again, told him she was busy and to relieve himself.

He came close to and stuck his face next to her ear. She could smell the perfume of another woman on his neck. Clearly, she wouldn't be the first he had been with that night. She saw red. After everything she had put up with, after all the beatings, after all the abuse, after all the anal sex she had been held down and forced to endure, he dared to sleep with another woman? Why? Was dominating and breaking his wife not enough for him? Did he need to humiliate her too?

She had gripped a butcher knife from the drawer and thought about cutting his throat. It would have taken mere seconds and he would have been gone. She could have easily claimed self-defense. God knew she had the bruises to prove it.

"I want it" he whispered into her ear. With that, he started caressing her inner thigh. When she pulled away, Brent grabbed her by the throat. Tightening his grip, he stared into her eyes. "You're my wife, don't tell me no." She gasped for air and it only helped to excite him.

Spinning her around, Sasha was shoved to the kitchen floor. Brent pulled at her pants and began to have his way with her. Like so many countless nights, Sasha dug her nails into the floor and cried. All she could do was wait for it to be over. But this time felt different. This time, something in her had changed. Thinking on it now, she wondered if it had been similar to how Sheriff Harrison had changed after coming home.

She was tired of the abuse. She was tired of the rape. She was tired of the humiliation. She was tired of lying to her daughter about the bruises. But above all, she was tired of a disgusting man treating her like a slave, no, an object. He fucked her and tossed her aside like a used napkin. Right there on the cold kitchen floor, she knew it would be his last screw. After tonight, he would never touch her again. With a plan forming in her mind, she began to grind back and forth with the illusion of pleasure. She wanted him to think he was breaking her in. It would make it all more worthwhile in the end.

Chapter Nine

Reluctantly, sheriff Harrison had announced the second death in the small town of Carlisle. They reacted much like a scared group of people would react. They panicked, they questioned authority, they demanded answers. Harrison couldn't give them the answers they wanted to hear, not yet. All he could do was reassure the killer would be caught and brought to justice.

However, there wasn't a single person he could even remotely accuse. He knew everyone in town and he couldn't believe any of them were capable of the crime. Of course, it couldn't be true. Someone had committed the murders but he hadn't the foggiest idea who. There seemed to be nothing to link the two victims together. It was almost as if the two crimes were completely random. The only link was the upside-down crosses. They had to mean something.

There was the obvious. Satanic ritual. But Harrison had his doubts. He suspected it was nothing more than subterfuge. Classic misdirection. Which meant, the killer was trying to hide something. Harrison was meant to focus on the possibility of the occult in order to miss something important. For Harrison, being cleverer than the killer gave him credit, it caused him to pay more attention to the little details. If it were meant to be a distraction then what was it distracting from?

Planted evidence was usually to frame an innocent party and throw suspicion away from the guilty. In this case, there was no one the imposed idea of devil worship implicated. It was an odd detail for sure. There wasn't a single person in town suspected of devil worship. It was the twenty-first century, after all. That kind of thing didn't exactly happen anymore.

The question burned in the back of his mind like a hot iron. What were the crosses for? Then there was the bone knife found at the second scene. It had to have been left for a reason, same as the victim's heart at Sasha's home.

A full set of prints had been lifted off the knife but he had no way of matching them locally. Instead, he forwarded a request to the FBI database in hopes they could come up with a match. It would take several days to get back but it would be done right. Normally, it would be an odd request for a local sheriff to enlist the help of the FBI in a simple murder case. But, being a war veteran had its perks and he still had friends in high places.

Harrison paced in his living room recounting the few facts he had. "Let's break this down," he said. "Ms. Shepard is stabbed in the forehead, presumably with the same knife as Ms. Granger, and upside-down crosses are painted on her cheeks in blood. Then, Ms. Granger is stabbed to death in the woods and her heart cut from her chest. The knife is tossed only a few yards from the body and the heart is left in Sasha's backyard. Again, upside-down crosses are drawn on Ms. Granger's cheeks.

I have to assume the knife and heart being left behind were not accidents. They were planted there with purpose, but why? Is Sasha involved somehow?" He doubted it before the sentence even left his mouth. "Is someone trying to frame her? No, that doesn't make sense. Why leave a piece of the body outside her home if they're trying to frame her. And the crosses wouldn't make any sense." He thought for a moment.

"Someone is trying to intimidate her. Wait, why the crosses?"

Whichever angle he viewed it from it was always cloudy. If only he could figure out what they meant. He felt like something was missing but couldn't quite put his finger on it. There had been something that stood out to him in Sasha's home but what was it?

"The black candle!" he yelled out loud. There had been one at the scene of Ms. Shepard and an identical one at Sasha's home. But a candle wasn't enough to link anything. For all he knew, it was a coincidence. And if it wasn't a coincidence, what could it possibly mean? What did a black candle signify?

"Witchcraft?" He wondered. Could that be the answer? Was someone trying to suggest Sasha was involved in witchcraft? It would explain the crosses, the ritualistic knife, the candles, and the removed heart. But why accuse her of witchcraft? No one in town knew her so why do anything? Maybe they wanted to isolate her from everyone, make her seem odd to the entire town? But why? Surely there'd be easier ways of going about it.

There seemed to be no answers to this case, only questions. In order to solve it, he needed to find the link between the symbolism and Sasha. He was certain the victims had been random. At the very least, a pattern had yet to be established. He hated the thought but he knew there would be no way of deciphering a pattern until another body was found. There would be more bodies before the killer was caught. Harrison was sure of it.

An idea slipped into the forefront of his mind. His next course of action should be to question the best source in town for news. Of course, he was thinking of the gossip ring which consisted of Josh Gruber- the town dentist, Betty Myer- a retired woman with too much time on her hands, Kyle Ferguson- who ran the drug store in the center of town, and Carol Leighter- who ran the local newspaper. The four of them were known about the town as the gossip group. Carol, on more than one occasion, used the Gossip Group as a source in one of her articles. They might have some insight to anyone acting strangely or out of the ordinary. Since the investigation was still open, he'd have to keep the details as vague as possible.

Grabbing his hat, Harrison climbed into the cab of his truck and sped off down the road. Gravel spewed out from under his tires and sprayed across his yard. Five minutes later, he was pulling in to Betty's driveway. He climbed out of the truck and trekked towards Betty Myer's home with purpose.

He pounded on the door and waited for an answer. There was the distinct sound of confused shuffling coming from inside before Betty answered the door. Harrison didn't wait for an invitation and proceeded to walk inside. Small town sheriff had its perks. If he did something he really shouldn't have, it didn't end up on every social media site within seconds. Harrison liked the freedom.

"Hey there, Sheriff." Kyle Ferguson said. "What can we do for you?"

Harrison smiled and removed his hat. He looked around at Ms. Myer's home. Every piece of décor hanging on the walls were older than Harrison, at least he guessed they were. The curtains were frilly and covered in a busy purple pattern. The yellow, dingy couch in the center of the living room was probably once vibrant and colorful. A thin layer of dust covered almost every inch of wooden furniture, giving it a more aged appearance.

"I need to know if you've heard anything around town."

"Is this about the murders?" Kyle asked.

"Yes and no" Harrison responded. "I can't give out the details but I need to know a few things."

"Like?" Betty asked.

"For starters, have any of you heard any disdain centered around the new woman, Sasha?"

"Does she have something to do with this?" Carol asked.

"No, no. Of course not. I just need to know if there's someone in town who doesn't like her, that's all."

The four of them looked at each other as if to seek approval. Finally, Josh said, "Nothing that we've heard of."

"Alright, keep me informed if you do hear anything. Report anything to me immediately. I'm serious. If anyone is having an issue with her, let me know."

They agreed and Harrison placed his hat back on his head. With that, he walked out of the home and back into his truck. The trip had been a complete bust. He was no closer to solving the case and he was almost certain he had started a rumor about Sasha by mistake. The end justified the means. If it brought the killer to justice then so be it.

• • • •

AFTER THE sheriff left, the Gossip Group started up instantly. They hollered and squawked like a flock of hungry seagulls. A new story had just fallen into their lap. It could be the front page of the paper. Newcomer Brings Murder from Big City. It practically wrote itself. This was the biggest thing to ever happen to their quiet little town.

They were saddened by the neighbors they had lost. It was a small community and everyone knew each other. Which meant all the more reason to bring this story to light. People needed to know the new woman in town brought them nothing but trouble. Would it panic the residents? Sure. But they needed to be scared, they should be scared. It would be foolish not to be.

Carol decided she would work on the article right away and have it on next morning's paper. Sheriff Harrison would be pissed but ultimately there was nothing he could do. Even in their small town, the Constitution still meant something. She had a right to report the news and that was just what she planned to do.

Chapter Ten

That night, the entire town of Carlisle slept uneasily. Each and every door remained locked and deadbolted with a fastened chain. Children slept snuggly in parent's bedrooms or in the living room as a family. It seemed no one wanted to be alone.

It was always hard for Sasha to sleep but tonight was much worse. Her anxiety levels were through the roof. Two dead bodies found in a town where murder had never happened could do that to a person. And all of this happened after she came to town, no less. It was enough to send the average person running for the hills. With Sasha's condition, she wondered if the hills would be far enough away. She couldn't even think about the heart found in her backyard without having a full-blown panic attack.

She wondered if they should pack up and leave but knew it wasn't that easy. Where would she go and with what money? Her mother had practically paid for the entire move. Sasha would soon need to provide herself with a stable income and she had yet to figure out how. The answers would come to her in time, she hoped. Until then, she had to stick it out. Desperately, she wanted this murder business to pass over the town. Perhaps the sheriff would catch the one responsible and it would all be over. But something deep down in her gut told her it wouldn't happen. For some reason, she felt she had a large part to play before it was all over. Attributing it to nothing more than sheer paranoia, Sasha attempted to sleep.

The next morning, she didn't feel rested at all. Had she not known better, she would have assumed she had only slept for an hour or two at most. The sunlight had filtered in through her bedroom window which would make it difficult for her to climb back in bed and try to feel rested. Instead, she would have to fight through the day with the feeling of utter exhaustion.

Drinking her morning coffee, Sasha sat down and flipped through yesterday's newspaper. It was a cute little thing which fit the atmosphere of the small town perfectly. Updates on locals, prices at the local market, what was new in town, and other stories littered the eight-page paper. She even found a small article about herself. A sort of welcome to the town. The gesture was sweet and she made a mental note to seek out the publisher and thank them for the article. At the top of the first page, she spotted Carol Leighter- Editor. she placed the paper down and sipped her coffee.

A knock at the front door broke the silence and sent a shiver down her spine. For some unknown reason, the thought of her ex-husband flashed through her mind. When the knock came again, she realized it had a certain urgency to it, though it was far from menacing. Pulling it open, she was greeted by the familiar and handsome face of Sheriff Harrison. His tough, bearded face gave her a sense of security and calm unlike any she had ever felt before. It was his eyes that told her he was strong. She could tell he would keep her safe if need be.

"I'm so sorry," he said as he held a newspaper in front of her face. There, on the front page, was a picture of her house with the tagline Newcomer Brings Murder from Big City. Sasha nearly fell to the floor. The name Carol Leighter was still printed in bold lettering next to the title of editor.

Sasha felt betrayed. A few seconds ago, she had thought to thank this Carol person. How could she have gone from a lovely letter of welcoming to one of such spite and fear? How could the murders be her fault and why would this woman want everyone to believe such a thing? Sasha had to fight back tears.

"This is all my fault," Harrison explained, seemingly reading her mind. "Yesterday, I spoke with the editor and her group. Around town, they're called The Gossip Group. I'm sure you can understand why. They can be a bit of a pain in the ass, but usually, they're harmless.

I had hoped what I asked her had been off the record. I guess I should have specified. I wish I hadn't gone to them. I'm so sorry."

"What the hell did you say to them?"

Harrison explained his thoughts as clearly as he could. Somehow, she was connected but he couldn't figure out how. He made sure to make it clear she was in no way a suspect. He believed someone might be targeting her to take the fall for the bodies. Of course, Sasha didn't take this news well.

"What do you mean someone's trying to pin this on me? What the hell did I do to anybody? I just got here. I was barely moved in before the first body hit the ground. What the hell is wrong with these people?"

"I know it doesn't mean much, and it doesn't make it right, but this is a small town. People here aren't used to change, nor do they welcome it. They see a new person like a threat to their way of life."

"So they set me up for murder?"

"Obviously, we're dealing with a very sick individual who needs help. What they're doing is wrong on many levels and I intend to stop them by any means necessary, I promise you. I thought hearing the news from a somewhat familiar face would make it a little easier to handle, rather than seeing it alone in the paper."

"I don't know that it does."

"Understandable. Would you like to get your daughter up and ready? I'd like to show you around a bit, maybe take your mind off things?"

Sasha thought about it for a moment, not sure what to say. The whole town would soon hate her. There was no telling how they would respond. Would they take up pitchforks and torches and run her out of town? Would some lone vigilante put her down, thinking it would end the killings? Fear changed people and turned them into ugly creatures, shells of their former selves. Sasha knew all too well.

"Yeah, sure. I guess I could use the distraction." What she really wanted to say was she felt safer staying with the sheriff than she did at home but he probably had been thinking the same thing. She told Harrison to make himself comfortable as she readied Tara for the day. Harrison wasted no time brewing himself a cup of coffee and sitting down on the couch with his feet up. He flipped through the morning paper while Sasha audibly struggled to get her daughter up and ready.

Sasha helped her daughter into the back seat of Sheriff Harrison's truck. When she was safely buckled in, Sasha moved up front with Sheriff Harrison. Harrison gave her a forced smile and turned the key over. They pulled away from Sasha's house and she watched it in the side mirror with a glint of sorrow in her eyes. Spending the day with the sheriff would be a great distraction but all she could think about was hiding under the covers in her bed.

While they drove, she admired the interior of Harrison's truck. It was well kept and clean. On the outside, it was a beat-up old truck with a few rusting parts. On the inside, it looked almost brand new. The beige seats were soft and smelled fresh. The carpet was free of stains and almost shone in the sunlight. Harrison must have shampooed them once a week. She guessed there was nothing better to do in town.

"First, let me show you my office," Harrison said. "In case you need to find me quickly, of course." He drove up to a rather small building painted an ugly brown color. Plastered on the door was a bright yellow sheriff badge. "Before you say anything, yes the building is ugly. No, I didn't pick it. And yes, I'm aware the yellow star on the front kind of looks like Nazi propaganda."

Sasha hadn't been thinking the last part but now she laughed. It was horrible, but the painted star on the door did look like the badge the Nazi's forced Jewish people to wear during their occupation of Germany. Had this been painted on a big city police station, it would have been all over social media in an instant. Protests and petitions would have forced the city to repaint. But in this quiet town, people left it alone.

"Ever thought about repainting?"

"Every day. But there's no budget for paint. I'm lucky if I can get enough bullets for my gun."

Sasha looked uneasy. How could a sheriff protect the town if he couldn't even afford bullets? Harrison must have sensed her worry and put them to rest. He said, "I'm only kidding. I actually buy bullets with my own money. Not that I've ever had a reason to fire a single shot."

"Now you might."

"Yeah."

He responded with what sounded like sorrow and regret. And why not? He knew everyone in town. Everyone was a friend, everyone was as close as family. One of those like-family members were killing the others. It must have been like finding out your child was a serial killer. You don't want to see them punished but you know in your heart they must be. Sasha couldn't even imagine.

She placed a reassuring hand on his arm and gave it a gentle squeeze. He gave her a brief smile and shrugged. "I'll do what I have to do."

"I know I don't know you well, yet, but I have a feeling you're going to do a fine job. I bet this town is lucky to have you." Internally, she berated herself for speaking the word yet. It had been so stupid. The implications of that word haunted her and she regretted it. But the hint of a small grin on his face eased her worry. Maybe he had enjoyed the word? Perhaps he enjoyed the subtle meaning behind its uttering. She wanted to know him better. She found him attractive. Could he possibly have deciphered that from one simple word? She thought so. He seemed an intelligent man.

"Look out your window there. You can see our water tower. The entire town's water supply is stored there. It draws water from a large, underground reservoir on a daily basis. From what I understand, the tower has to resupply daily as each gallon is used. You wouldn't think such a small town goes through so much water. I guess we're very *thirsty*."

Now it was her turn to notice the upward inflation, or had she imagined it? Sasha was certain the sheriff was flirting with her but could not be sure. The thought was a welcome escape from her normal life. It had been many years, since high school in fact, since a man had given her the feeling of fluttering butterflies in her stomach. She felt juvenile. She felt free.

Brent had never made her feel like a woman. He never bought her flowers, never told her how beautiful she looked, and didn't even try to flirt with her. To him, she was nothing more than an object. He abused her and used her body for his sexual needs. She was nothing but a dumpster. And that dumpster was his property.

A man had once made the mistake of calling her beautiful at a bar one night. Flattered, Sasha thanked the man and hid the blush which had broken out across her face. Since that particular compliment was scarce in her own life, she couldn't help but accept it. She needed some form of positive reinforcement in her life and if it had to come from a stranger then so be it.

But Brent was none too happy. He had leaned out from behind Sasha and yelled at the man, the beer on his breath wafting into her face. Brent was vicious and angry but the other man merely laughed him off. He added insult to injury when he told Brent to go to the bathroom and splash a little water on his face to cool off. Brent's embarrassing response had been, "Oh, I am cool, buddy. Far cooler than you. You're gonna be jerking it tonight with nothing but your tears as lube and I'm gonna fuck this woman so hard she won't walk straight for a week." Of course, Brent found it hilarious but Sasha found it disgusting and humiliating. All the other women in the bar made faces at them, some of them laughed. She couldn't take it anymore. Sasha stormed away. Before she made it out the door, she heard the man say, "Guess you'll be using your tears tonight, buddy." The bar had a good laugh. Even Sasha felt a smirk touch her hot face, though she did her best to hide it.

Brent was furious now. He stood up and approached the man, hell-bent on teaching him some sort of lesson. To this day, Sasha regretted what she had done next. She had dragged Brent out of the bar and to the car, stopping the fight before it started. She wondered what would have happened had she let him fight the man. He was young, he was in good shape, and he didn't seem the least bit frightened of Brent. Maybe he could have taught Brent a lesson that night. Who knows, maybe it would have given Sasha the courage to leave him and ended up with a man who truly appreciated her. It could have been the man at the bar for all she knew.

No, instead she endured a rage-fueled car ride home as he screamed at her for allowing another man to hit on her. As if it were her fault a man had called her beautiful. Clearly, she had been flirting to get his attention. He belittled her and stripped away all of her worth. Then, he established his dominance over her like he had so many countless nights before. As usual, tears rolled down Sasha's cheeks and she could do nothing but dig her nails into the pillow in front of her.

Now, she looked over at Harrison and saw the man at the bar. He seemed calm, even with everything happening in town. Sasha thought he knew how to treat a woman right, with respect and dignity. And, above all else, he did not seem like an abuser. Sasha would never go back. It would never happen to her again. Not after everything she had done to get away from Brent. There was no going back for her, ever. Sasha had done what she never thought she could to escape the clutches of that terrible man. No one but her mother knew her secret. Sasha had murdered her ex-husband.

Chapter Eleven

She knew she could never leave her husband. The first time she had threatened to leave him was also the last time she threatened it. The fight had escalated beyond anything she thought possible. He fell into a mad panic and lashed out with an open palm. The smack was so hard it busted her bottom lip open. After that, she was thrown to the ground like garbage.

He had tried to force her legs apart but Sasha attempted to hold firm. He smacked her groin over and over until it bruised. Finally, she had relented and opened her legs. While he did his deed, he gritted his teeth in her face. "You belong to me," he said. "If you ever leave me I will find you. I'll do worse than this to you. I'll fucking kill any man you're with. Fuck, I'll even have Tara."

"That's your daughter!" she cried but Brent only smacked her in the face.

"You shut up and stay still. I like my pussy silent."

Sasha knew divorce was out of the question. Did she really believe he would do as he promised? She wasn't sure. But she couldn't put her daughter in jeopardy like that. Watching her mom get hit was one thing but getting raped by her father, that would destroy her life. Years of therapy would hardly help her. In the end, she would end up with the same mental disorder her mother suffered from. Probably much worse. It wasn't a risk Sasha was willing to take.

She loathed the man for all of the things he had ever done to her but threatening her daughter was the worst. There was no chance of redemption for him. He was a disgusting pile of human waste and she would dispose of him as such.

He continued with his outbursts and she continued to take his beatings. His days were numbered. It was easier to take the abuse when you knew it wouldn't last much longer. Under the lie of grocery shopping, Sasha took her daughter to the library. Tara grabbed a handful of books and found a nice quiet corner to read.

Sasha went about some research. Particularly, ways to kill someone without leaving a trace. Using a library computer was the best way she knew to keep her search history clear. If she was ever suspected of murder, they wouldn't be able to prove premeditation at least.

She came across many articles that talked about the decomposition of the human body and the best methods of cleaning the scene so no trace could be found. But it was all from a professional standpoint. Something a crime scene investigator would use. She wanted the good stuff. She wanted advice on how to secretly kill someone.

It took several months, and countless trips to the library, to finally come up with the best method. The answer seemed so obvious. Poison. If done correctly, an autopsy could completely miss it. It could be mistaken for a heart attack, especially in heavier set victims with high cholesterol. It fit Brent perfectly. But, she had to be careful with the poison. Certain ones could be suspicious. Others could be found in the body naturally. Then there was the small issue of getting her hands on the right material.

During her research, she learned a car battery could become a source of poison. She simply needed a tub of water, a car battery, and a knife. If she could puncture the battery, she could then submerge it in the water and begin to serve the tainted drink to her husband. It would take several agonizing days to die but eventually, he would. She liked the idea and almost ran to Wal-Mart to buy a battery before realizing the major flaw. He never drank water. If she tried to force it on him, the plan might backfire. The beatings could get worse. He might even kill her or Tara. It wasn't worth the risk. Though she liked the thought of making him suffer for days, she wanted something quicker.

She flipped through countless articles and posts outlining poisons and how they worked. Several seemed like a good idea but most were hard to come by. She had no seedy connections so anything illegal would be out. There had to be something which could be legally obtained and used as a poison. There had to be.

Then, she found it. The light in her mind clicked on with the realization of success. A little plant called Belladonna. It was perfect. The plant itself was highly toxic. Just a handful of berries could kill a human being. The name itself was perfect, too. Belladonna was Italian meaning beautiful lady. Could there be a more perfect cosmic justice by which to end his life? Sasha thought not.

Finding the berries or even the plant would be difficult. Though they were not illegal in the United States, she couldn't find any way to buy the berries in her area. Brent would never allow her to head off on a road trip by herself. He would probably assume she was off to meet some boyfriend and she would find herself on the wrong end of another beating. No. She had to have the poison come to her. The perfect idea seemed to be slipping from her fingers.

Performing a search for *Belladonna* online provided her with some useful information. She could buy a bottle of Belladonna extract on eBay. Better yet, she found a few local alternative medicine shops in town. She could buy a bottle in cash. That would be her best option. Having a bottle of poison delivered to her home via eBay seemed like the easiest way to get caught.

One day, while her husband was at work, Sasha took Tara to her mother's and asked her to watch her for a couple of hours. She then went about the task of planning the murder. Before she arrived at the store, she wondered if she would back out. In the end, she had not. Sasha walked into the store and found the bottle she was looking for, slipped her cash across the counter, and walked out with her head high. Change was coming.

She let a few days pass before putting her plan into action. It would be simple. Sasha would simply bring her husband a beer. He never turned them down. He would drink one, then another, and another. Sometime after he had become inebriated, she would hand him the last beer he would ever drink. It would have the entire bottle of Belladonna secretly inside the beer. He would toss his head back and down the drink without question and without taste. After the seventh or eighth beer, he stopped tasting them. At that point, he was only drinking to maintain intoxication.

The plan worked smoothly. She handed him the first beer and watched with anticipation as he drank it down. Quickly, she readied another. This went on for a couple of hours before she felt confident enough to give him the tainted drink. Her hands shook as she poured the drug into his beer. The medicine was a dark brown color and would have turned a normal lager into a disgusting, brownish mess. Fortunately, for Sasha, Brent preferred to drink ales. They were dark and bitter. Sasha had sipped one once and nearly puked in the sink. How any human being could ingest it was beyond her. Now, she was thankful for the beautiful, disgusting drink.

Brent downed the glass without so much as a second thought. He belched and laughed, seemingly pleased with himself. Sasha smirked and removed the glass from his hand. A flutter of excitement and shame passed through her body simultaneously. There was no going back now. The poison would kill him and she would then hide the body. It was self-defense, she kept telling herself. The torture would never stop. The abuse would never end. This was the only way.

After a few hours, Sasha began to worry. Nothing seemed to happen. Maybe she had misjudged the drug. It wasn't as potent as she thought. Now, she'd have to start over and find something new. Perhaps the car battery would be the best option, though she had no idea how she would make it work. Before she could mentally prepare for a new course of action, something began to happen to Brent.

It started with his hands. They convulsed in rapid succession, seemingly smacking at invisible flies. Foam lathered around his mouth and his body shook in uncontrollable spasms. A disturbing choking sound bellowed from his throat. Shortly after, a wheezing sound kicked in. His eyes darted back and forth like he was seeing something that wasn't there and he sunk down low in his chair. The entire time, he continued to spasm and convulse. The scene was horrible. She watched him to the very last spasm. When he finally stopped moving, she knew it was all over. Finally, the threat was gone.

Needing to be sure he was gone, Sasha pressed two shaky fingers against his neck. When she didn't feel a pulse, she knew it had worked. Disposing of the body would be her next trick. She had read about acid baths that could dissolve a human body. Online advice had also instructed to chop the body to pieces and destroy anything that could identify the body. Smash the teeth, burn off fingerprints, cut out the eyes, and everything in between. But these methods were too messy and gruesome. Instead, she decided it would be best to bury the body in the woods far away from her home. He would never be found. Heat increased the speed of decomposition and it was currently the hottest time of year. Hopefully, he would be reduced to nothing in no time. A couple of days after burying him, she would report him missing. Maybe he ran off with some whore he met at a bar. They'd believe it. Even if they suspected foul play, there was no proof.

As she had planned, Sasha loaded the body in the trunk of her car and drove several miles out of state. Tara had already been dropped off at Grandma's house long before. She would be staying there for the time being.

Sasha's mother had not taken the news well. Of course, she had wanted a better life for Sasha than that of an abused spouse but her problems had grown exponentially. Tara could be left without parents if she were ever caught. Sasha insisted they would never find the body, they would never find out it was her. What proof could they possibly get? Without a body, there's no cause of death. Sure, maybe there would be speculation she had killed her husband but it wouldn't matter. No proof, no prison. It was simple. They'd never find the body, she was sure of it.

Reluctantly, her mother decided to help her by watching Tara and agreeing to loan her as much money as she could afford to move away after everything blew over. There was an investigation but the police never came up with any leads. It was the longest couple of months of Sasha's life. Her anxiety had gone into overdrive. She hardly slept, she barely ate. Every waking moment she feared would be her last as a free woman.

When the case went unsolved, and the detective involved informed her the most likely scenario had been abandonment, Sasha was then able to move out of town. She had put on a good show for the detective. Her heart was broken, she couldn't stand to stay in the same city, let alone the same house, as her missing husband. She needed to leave.

There was not a single ounce of regret on her mind. She had killed her husband, yes, but Sasha felt it was more in self-defense. A jury might not see it that way but it was what she had done. Ultimately, she did an unspeakable act in order to keep herself and her daughter safe. Sasha was certain she could live with that.

A few weeks later and she found herself in the small town of Carlisle. Maybe one day she would be able to return to her old life, take Tara back to her friends. Maybe one day she would be able to stop looking over her shoulder, expecting the police to be standing there.

Chapter Twelve

Sheriff Harrison had taken her mind off of the murders, her name in the paper, and even her husband. But now, back at home, the broken levy of memories flooded back like a tidal wave. The dark secret she swore to take to her grave was screaming to come out. For the briefest moment, she thought about sharing the burden with Harrison. Perhaps he would understand.

It was a ridiculous thought and she knew it. She had killed Brent to protect herself from his wickedness. But the law wouldn't be on her side. Which meant, Sheriff Harrison wouldn't be on her side. She couldn't bear to tell another human being what she had done. Telling her mother had been hard enough. Though her mother protected and helped her, Sasha knew her mother secretly despised her. She had committed murder. No matter what angle it was viewed from, it was murder.

Sasha understood how her mother felt. It was how she felt about herself. There was no doubt in her mind she had done what she needed to survive. There was no escaping that man and his abuse. Running would have delayed the inevitable. Action had been necessary. Had she stayed with Brent, she would have been killed sooner or later. Whether it be on purpose or on accident, she knew she would have been killed. Perhaps it would have been a push down the stairs or the cold steel of a kitchen knife against her throat. Either way, her time would have been short.

She kicked off her shoes and fell down on the couch. The day had brought a myriad of emotions and exhausted her to the core. She ran a hand through her hair and looked around the room. Something seemed off, though she couldn't quite place what it was. After a few moments of thought, she realized a few items were slightly askew. Like the throw blanket on the back of the couch. It had been folded nicely and hung with care. Now, it lay in a heap on the floor.

Maybe it was just her imagination and nothing was out of place. The blanket on the floor could have had a simple explanation. A breeze from the open front door may have blown it off the back of the couch. Or, perhaps more simply, it had fallen when she let herself fall on the couch. But of course, nothing about her situation was normal. Everything seemed strange. She had murdered her husband, fled her life, found a home in the middle of nowhere in a town she had never heard of. None of it felt right.

It took a moment to sink in, but eventually, she noticed something was actually missing. The black candle she had found while unpacking was gone. She was certain she had left it on the end table and it was no longer there. At first, panic had set in like a burning fire deep inside her soul. Every appendage tingled with terror. Had someone been in her house? Had someone stolen the black candle? Was it the killer? Why?

Of course, she did have a kid in the house. They were apt to grab things and move them without so much as a reason. When Tara had been a toddler, she had refused to stop picking up her mother's shoes and throwing them about the house. No matter how hard Sasha spanked her and how many times Brent yelled, Tara continued her escapade. Deciding it must be the answer, she headed off towards Tara's room to investigate. Slowly, she creaked open her daughter's bedroom door. Tara sat on the floor playing with one of her favorite dolls. Sasha smiled at her daughter and decided she didn't want to disturb her. Instead of asking, Sasha glanced around the room but found nothing.

Quickly, she shut the door and darted back to the living room. She snatched up her cell phone and dialed the sheriff's number. It seemed silly, calling about a missing candle but it had to mean something. The body found near her home and the heart in her backyard had made her understandably jumpy. Whoever had taken the candle from her home may have been the same person who cut out the heart. In her mind, there was no doubt.

"Goddamnit, of course." She yelled. "No signal when I need it."

Dialing again, she did not notice Tara come out of her room. "Son of a bitch!" Sasha yelled and spun around to meet her daughter's gaze. Immediately, she dropped the phone and forced a smile.

"Is something wrong, Mommy?"

Sasha shook her head. There was no need to fill her daughter's head with suspicion and fear. She had seen enough in her short life. Things were supposed to be different here in Carlisle. This was supposed to be a fresh start for her, for both of them. If it couldn't be for Sasha she would make damn sure it was for Tara, no matter what.

"Of course not, sweetheart. The stupid phone just isn't working. That's all." She prayed her daughter would buy the bluff.

"Ok." Tara turned around and went back to her room, leaving Sasha to breathe a sigh of relief. But her panic wasn't over yet. She still needed to get a hold of Harrison. Then, she remembered the slip of paper he had given her. His address! The phone might not work but she could drive to his place. Getting out of the house would help to clear her mind. Knowing someone had entered her home drummed up feelings of violation and being there only served to make it worse.

"Tara, sweetie, would you mind getting your shoes on? We have to make a quick trip." Her daughter called out in acknowledgement a few seconds later. Sasha grabbed her keys and led Tara out of the house. Her cell phone rested on the back of the couch where she had slammed it down. Sasha had completely forgotten about it.

• • • •

STANDING IN the cover of darkness, a hooded figure watched as Sasha loaded her little girl into the car and tore out of the driveway. The hooded figure watched long past Sasha's departure. It stood there, staring at the house almost as if it would do a trick if watched long enough. Finally, after ten minutes had passed, the hooded figured stepped from the shadows and marched across the street towards the house.

• • • •

SASHA PULLED into Harrison's driveway and flicked off the headlights. Being at the sheriff's home made her feel foolish. After all, it had only been a candle. There were a thousand explanations for where it might have been. Was it really important enough to disturb the sheriff so late in the evening? And on his own doorstep no less. She told the familiar doubting voice in the back of her mind to be quiet. It always doubted her. Tonight, she would not listen to it. Tonight, she would be making the calls. There was a killer out there somewhere. She had to keep her daughter safe.

She pounded on the door and tapped her foot on the concrete below. Tara stood nervously by, staring at her mother in bewilderment. There was nothing Sasha could have said to Tara at that moment which would have made sense. Instead, she remained quiet.

Harrison opened the door in jeans and a plain, white tee shirt. He stared at Sasha in confusion. Then he perked up like he saw something in her eyes. "What is it? What's wrong?" Sasha pulled her daughter in front of her like a shield.

"Can we come in?"

"Of course." He gestured them inside and shut the door, but not before scanning the darkness behind them.

"Please, have a seat." He said and Sasha did. "Would you like-"

"Someone was in my house."

"What?"

"I mean, they *were* in my house. Not while we were in it, well not that I know of, but someone had been there."

"Wait, slow down. What are you talking about?"

"Someone was in my house."

"Yeah, I got that part."

"Something was missing, Harrison. They broke in and took something. I don't know why they did. It was just a stupid candle. Why would someone want to steal a black candle?"

"Did you say a black candle?"

Sasha nodded.

"I found it in the end table after we unpacked. I thought it was weird looking but it smelled pretty nice. Why would someone take it?"

Harrison turned towards Tara. "Hey there, sweetheart. Would you mind giving your mother and I a moment? You can go to my room and watch cartoons on my TV."

"Ok."

"Thank you. It's the last door on the right. Can't miss it."

Tara got up and headed to the bedroom, rubbing her eyes. Sasha felt bad for her. She could see the exhaustion in her daughter's eyes and she felt awful for being the reason she was still awake. What was worse, it may have all been for nothing. Just her overactive imagination and frazzled nerves. God, she hoped it was that simple. Nothing would please her more than to find out the candle had been knocked under the couch or Tara had hidden it in her room.

"Sasha, this candle, was it solid black?"

She nodded.

"And you found it in your house?"

Again, she nodded.

"You're absolutely sure it's missing?"

"Jesus, yes. I looked everywhere for it. What's with this candle? Please, tell me what's going on, Harrison. I'm scared out of my mind here."

"There was something I left out of the report concerning the first murder. The killer left behind some markings which made the scene seem satanic. I believe it's a ruse to throw me off the trail. But, there was a solid black candle found next to the body. Sounds like it might be exactly like the one you found."

"What the hell was it doing in my home?"

"I don't know but what worries me more is why it was stolen."

"What do you mean?"

"One was found at a murder scene. Odds are, it was stolen to be used at another."

Sasha's blood ran cold.

"How did the killer know I had one?"

Harrison shook his head.

"I can't go back there tonight," Sasha said, scooting closer to Harrison on the couch. She hoped he would catch the major signal she was sending. *Please let me stay at your house tonight.* Harrison grabbed her shoulder and gave it a reassuring squeeze.

"Don't you worry. You and Tara can stay here tonight."

"You don't have to do that." *Oh, thank you, God.*

"I do, though, don't I? Serve and protect, right? I figure this is doing both."

She had to hold herself back from flinging her arms around his neck and holding him tight. There was no way she could go back to that house tonight. She would sit up all night and be petrified of every little noise and thought. It wasn't even herself she was worried for but Tara. If she lost her, well, she didn't even want to think about it.

"You and Tara can have my bed if you'd like. I'll take the couch."

"Oh, no, I couldn't. It's your house."

"Don't worry about it. I spend most nights on the couch as it is. That big bed feels too, empty."

Sasha tried to read his remark, wondering if there was an invitation there. Was he hinting he wanted to share a bed with her? God, how she hated these games. It was so hard to tell when someone was interested or just being friendly.

"Thank you so much, Harrison. I don't think I could ever repay you for your kindness."

"Call me David and we'll be even." He gave her a friendly smile. Sasha smiled back.

"Sure thing, David."

David Harrison led her down the hall and to the bedroom. Opening the door, they found Tara sprawled across the bed, her hair everywhere. Sasha couldn't even think about disturbing her at the moment. She desperately needed her sleep.

Turning to David, she said, "I think I should give her a little while longer. I don't want to wake her up."

"Maybe if you come back in, say, an hour, she'll have moved?"

"Exactly."

"Well, you're more than welcome to join me on the couch. I'll put something on and we can relax."

"Sure."

But Sasha didn't give him time to get to a remote. Something in her came to life. She couldn't explain it but she felt more courage now than she had in years. Harrison made her feel the butterflies she had not felt in ages. He treated her well, he lent her a helping hand, and he never made her feel like an object. She realized the irony of throwing herself at the man made her exactly that but she didn't care. It would be a welcomed distraction.

Straddling his lap, Sasha began to kiss him passionately. He ran his fingers through her hair and he did the same. Seconds later, the two of them tangled together on the couch in a full display of passion. The two of them fondled and caressed each other's naked bodies with only a small glint of starlight filtering through the windows to see. They were caught up with each other and neither noticed the hooded figure watching them from the corner of the living room window.

Chapter Thirteen

Across town from the cuddled-up Harrison and Sasha slept a woman alone in her bed. She tossed and turned trying to get comfortable. Her boyfriend was out of town visiting his mother. She was growing older and he wanted to spend as much time with her as possible. She knew she could never ask him to stay home and keep her company over visiting his family back home. Desiree wished she, herself, had fit in more time with her own mother before she had died.

Life had caused Desiree and her mother to grow apart. Like a lot of people, she had grown up and moved away. After her mother died, she felt guilty for spending so little time with her in her adult life. Her boyfriend, Grant, had always told her not to feel guilty. Her mother knew she loved her very much. Though, it never made her feel better.

Desiree sat up in bed and looked around. The bed was cold and empty without Grant. The room felt quieter than usual. The whole house did. She missed his body heat wrapping tightly around her like a cocoon. His nude body only inches from hers. More often than not, their sleeping in the nude kept them from truly sleeping. Their sex life was good, excellent in fact. Almost every night before bed they embrace each other in passion. Thinking about it excited her and formed an idea to help her sleep.

Making love to Grant always seemed to help her sleep. When he was gone, she always had trouble. She wondered why this idea had never occurred to her before. If Grant wasn't there to take care of her, she'd just have to do it herself.

She climbed out of bed and didn't bother with any clothing. The cool air in the house felt amazing on her silky smooth, bare skin. Desiree flicked on the bathroom light and bent down to search under the sink. It was hidden in the far corner of the sink cabinet, underneath a few items. She wanted to make sure no one ever discovered it by mistake. Not even Grant knew about her little toy. Whenever he was out of the house and she pulled it out, she got a twinge of excitement. Almost as if she had taken on a lover.

Desiree pulled the silver, bullet-shaped vibrator from the box and headed back towards the bedroom. She stopped in her tracks and glanced around the dark house. Although she couldn't be certain, she swore she had heard heavy breathing. Listening intently, she heard nothing. Jumping at shadows, that's all it was. Her imagination was starting to run wild. Soon, she would only care about the silver bullet.

From the darkness behind her, a gloved hand shot out and slapped over her mouth. A second hand cupped her exposed breast. Desiree's eyes began to bulge in absolute terror. She kicked and flailed, helplessly. Her attacker was strong. Every fiber of her being screamed for her to break free and run. Something terrible was about to happen.

His gloved hand searched up and down her body forcefully as tears rolled down her face. This had to be some sort of horrible nightmare. She would wake up in a cold sweat and everything would be fine. But it *felt* real. She knew it was real. And she had a terrible feeling this would be the last moment of her life.

• • • •

HARRISON FELT the bile rise in his throat but he forced it back down. It was a scene, unlike anything he had ever seen before. He vowed to bring the person responsible to justice, whatever that meant. Harrison preferred it to mean a bullet from his gun. The awful scene before him did nothing but fill him with rage.

On the floor lay the body of Desiree Cortez. Disturbingly, she was not in one piece. Her legs had been spread so wide they had dislocated from their sockets. It gave her an eerie configuration, almost inhuman. Her tongue had been removed and now rested in a drying pool of blood only a few feet from the body. Several fingers and toes were missing. The killer may have taken them as a memento. Harrison had searched everywhere for the missing digits to no avail. There was evidence of multiple stab wounds. One, disturbingly enough, had been delivered to her right eye. The bloody crosses were present on her cheeks, much like the others before. Unlike before, these crosses had been carved. Harrison wouldn't be sure until after an autopsy but he had the strong suspicion the woman had been raped before the end, perhaps even after the end. Harrison had found something silver under the couch and had rolled it out with a pencil. It was a shiny, silver vibrator slick with blood.

The scene was almost unbearable. Only one thing seemed clear. The killer had been in a rage when killing Desiree. Her left eye fared better than her right, having not been stabbed, but not by much. It was swollen and bruised and looked like the killer had delivered several powerful strikes. Purple welts covered her abdomen and arms. The last two deaths had been brutal, yes, but seemed relatively quick. For some unknown reason, the killer had been whipped into a frenzy. Harrison feared for his town now. It was bad enough having a killer in their midst, but this? This was inhuman. This was disturbing. This had to be stopped.

As Harrison squatted next to the body, he spotted something across the room in the far corner. He stood up and approached the object, taking great care not to touch it. Again, with his pencil, he tugged at the black mass. It was a candle, much like the one found with the first body. It may have even been the one Sasha had lost. It slipped free of his pencil and toppled to the floor. He let it roll a few feet away without stopping it. There wasn't a chance in hell he would risk contaminating whatever fingerprints might be on the candle. Beyond any DNA left on, or disgustingly, inside the body, it was their only chance of evidence.

When the candle came to a stop, Harrison noticed something carved into the side. From the angle, he could see two letters. S A. Harrison turned the candle with his pencil and read the five little letters that nearly stopped his heart. S-A-S-H-A.

"What the fuck?" Harrison nearly shouted. Framing her was no longer the goal. This was an outright death threat. Someone in town was warning her. They wanted her gone. Harrison had had enough. He couldn't understand how someone could do all of this over something so simple as a newcomer. Rape and dismemberment? Who in town could do something so twisted and so vile? There was no one he could think of whom was mentally unstable. Not to the degree this crime had insinuated.

But there was a bigger problem at stake. If the town knew the severity of this crime, and the branded candle, a panic would surely surge through the town like lightning. There was a difficult choice ahead, no matter how Harrison proceeded. The town needed him, now more than ever. They trusted him. With a killer terrorizing the community, people were already panicked. To let loose the details of the black candle bearing Sasha's name would only condemn her. The town already distrusted her. Though most people in town might not have truly believed Sasha was the killer, they surely thought her to be the catalyst. The clock was ticking. Soon, the town would either run her out or worse.

Which brought him back to his current dilemma. He had two choices laid out before him. Either, he would hide certain details about the case in order to protect Sasha or he would force her to leave to protect the town. Hiding the details might spare Sasha from being run out of town but the killings would continue. If she were gone, they might stop. Of course, there was no guarantee of anything and he couldn't lie to himself. His feelings for her were getting in the way of making the choice. It seemed the right decision would be to send her away.

However, Harrison didn't believe that. Sure, the killer might stop. But for how long? Once a killer, always a killer. Eventually, they would get thirsty for it again. The bodies would start up again and he would be right back where he started, only without Sasha. No, sending her away would be a band-aid to a gaping wound.

He started to despise himself for even thinking about casting Sasha away like a piece of waste. Thanks for the sex, now get out of my town and take your murdering stalker with you! It was out of the question.

His mind was made up. The candle would be left out of the official report. He would be the only one to know the truth.

He was thankful no one had stumbled across the crime scene before it had been reported. Instead, Harrison had received an early morning call from Brian Anderson, one of her neighbors, stating Desiree was not answering the door. Brian was the local groundskeeper and always took care of Desiree's yard, and almost everyone else's in town for that matter. He knew her morning routine better than anyone else. When she didn't answer, he knew something was wrong.

He scheduled a pick up for Desiree's body and went about collecting the evidence. With a plastic bag, he snatched up the black candle and stuffed it under the seat in his truck. It felt wrong but it was the only option. There was no time to worry about it, however. He needed to find a way to address the town and avoid the inevitable panic this death would cause. A curfew or some form of martial law might be the answer but he was unsure. Harrison knew he had a hard time ahead of him. He had no idea how much worse it was all going to get.

Chapter Fourteen

"If you know something, say something," Harrison said from the town hall stage. With another body found, he had decided to call another town meeting. Of course, he left out certain details such as the candle and Sasha's carved name. There was no need to further implicate her in a crime she clearly had nothing to do with.

The crowd murmured together as everyone talked amongst themselves. "Together, we can put a stop to these horrific crimes. That's why I'm urging anyone with any information to come see me directly. Someone here knows something and it's your responsibility to speak up, even if you don't think it's important. If someone you know is spending time out of the house at odd hours of the night, I need to know about it. Every little detail counts here, people."

"Investigate the new woman," a voice cried out. Several other voices shouted out in agreement. Sasha, sitting in the back of the room, could only shrink down so low. If the room erupted into a violent mob and turned on her, which seemed quite likely, she wanted to be as well out of sight as possible.

"People, get a hold of yourselves," Harrison boomed over the increasing noise. "At this time, we don't have any suspects. If anyone has a reason to suspect someone, bring it to me in private."

"None of this happened until she came to town. That's reason enough for me!" A voice cried out.

"Yeah, she brought it with her from the city. I read it in the paper!" Another yelled.

"Jesus Christ," Harrison whispered, not entirely sure if everyone had heard him or not. "People, please. We might be a small town, but the constitution is still in effect here. Everyone is still innocent until proven guilty. Now, I don't want to hear any more baseless accusations. If you have hard-"

A voice cried out from the crowd, "I say you arrest her just to be safe. What harm would it do?" This seemed to spark the attention of the crowd. Many whispered their agreeance. Others clapped and some cheered. Harrison's blood began to boil. They were scared, he understood as much. But the accusations were wildly unfounded. There was nothing which connected Sasha to the crime scenes. At least, nothing the town was aware of. At that moment, Harrison knew he had made the right decision. This town hall meeting would have taken a violent turn had they known Sasha was somehow connected to it all.

"People, I can guarantee Sasha is not involved in these killings. She has a strong alibi which proves she was nowhere near Desiree's home during the time of the murder."

"So, you've questioned her?" Carol Leighter's voice called out. "Does that mean she *was* a suspect?"

Harrison shook his head, growing tired of the questioning. The meeting was not going at all how he had planned. Opposition was to be expected, sure. But these people were being blind, no ignorant. They didn't want the truth, they wanted a scapegoat. To think someone from their innocent, small town could be capable of such atrocities was a hard truth to swallow. Instead, it was easier to blame the outsider. Harrison wanted hard evidence. He wanted to convict a murderer. Instead, he was having to defend a woman he already knew to be innocent.

"Carol, I need you to pull it back a bit with the articles. You're scaring the town. We have no leads and we have no suspects."

"So, you're saying it could be her?"

"No, I'm saying we need evidence before we act on anything. If you have something that incriminates her then bring it to me. Otherwise, trust me when I tell you she had nothing to do with last night's murder."

This circus had to come to an end. The fact that Sasha hadn't stormed out of the town hall already was a miracle. Though, Harrison feared how her doing so would make her look to the town. It was time to rope all of this in before real harm was done.

"And why not?" Carol persisted.

"My God, Carol. Please, let's drop the questions. I need you to be my eyes out there. You can't be working against me here."

"Then just tell me how she couldn't be involved in Desiree's murder!"

"I told you all, Desiree was sexually assaulted by the attacker. A woman could not have physically done it."

"Or, maybe she has someone working with her."

"Oh, for the love of, fine. Sasha couldn't have done it because she was at my home last night."

Before the words had lifted from his tongue, he regretted them. His face went red and he assumed Sasha's had done the same. Sheriff Harrison held his breath and waited for the inevitable collapse. Almost the entire town suspected the new woman in town to have killed their friends and neighbors and now they knew the sheriff had slept with her.

Sasha stood up and pulled her daughter out of the building. Harrison thought about running after her but decided it was pointless. He had done enough to embarrass her. There would be time to talk to her later. Now, there was damage control to be done. The room was still quiet and everyone shifted uneasily in their chairs. Most stared at him and others looked at each other. Finally, the room exploded with voices. They boomed from every corner. Harrison did his best to listen for anything he could answer, anything rational.

"I don't feel safe anymore. I'm afraid to even leave my house. What are you doing about it, sheriff?"

"You people turned this into a zoo. All I wanted was cooperation and assistance to catch the one responsible for these horrible crimes. While you all proceeded with your little witch hunt, someone is planning to take another life. Focusing on the new woman, whose name is Sasha by the way, is getting us nowhere."

The murmuring turned to a dull roar as everyone exploded at once. It was no use trying to quite them down. Harrison had lost all control. Fear had gripped the small town and pulled them deeper into the dark abyss of chaos. Fear could make people do unspeakable things and Harrison now feared for the future of the town and worse, Sasha.

The murmuring quickly turned hostile and people began yelling and screaming. Harrison had to break up one fight which nearly broke out in front of the stage. He yelled for the crowd to calm down but no one seemed to hear him. It was only a matter of seconds before the group formed an angry mob and ran Sasha out of town.

"Harrison is right," a woman screamed from atop her chair. The phrase had stopped everyone in their tracks, including the sheriff. Everyone stopped in an instant and stared at the woman. The woman looked around at the crowd and wagged her finger. Harrison looked down at her and nodded.

"Thank you, Mrs. Hazel."

Her husband had died a few years ago but that didn't stop everybody from calling her Mrs. She preferred it actually. After the loss of her husband, she had become something of a hermit. Rarely did she venture out of her home and when she did, she always had statements to say which made her seem unbalanced. Harrison took pity on her, fearing it might be early stages of dementia. Now, he wasn't so sure.

"The sheriff is right. It's a witch hunt people, open your damn eyes. That witch has cursed this town. Slowly, she's killing us all." Harrison listened to the woman ramble longer than he should have, nearly dropping the mic in surprise.

"Oh, fuck." It was all Harrison could mutter.

No one said a word for nearly a minute. Many were silent out of disbelief and uncertainty of how to respond. Others seemed to be nodding in agreement. Sheriff Harrison thought about praying to God, asking him to send these people common sense. But he knew it would do no good. Like the townspeople, he wasn't listening.

"It's why she keeps the curtains closed at her house," Mrs. Hazel continued. "She practices her dark magic there and dances with Satan in the trees. The woman is a witch from hell. Mark my words."

"Mrs. Hazel, this is ridiculous. I need you to-"

"What if she's on to something?" Carol Leighter blurted out. Harrison, who couldn't think of anything to say, rolled his eyes. "Seriously, sheriff, think about it. The symbols found on the bodies, the black candle at the first scene, even the knife found with the second body. It all seems to point to one conclusion."

"Oh, you've got to be kidding me. I have no idea what you're talking about." Harrison said.

"Please, Harrison. I saw the police report myself."

"How the hell did you get this information?"

"I can't give out my sources."

It was Donald, one of his deputies, he knew it was. The man was an idiot. All Carol had to do was come into the precinct, show a little interest in him and he fell apart. Harrison would have fired him years ago if his father wasn't on the city council. Granted city council was only two people, they still held power.

"If you do anything like that again, Carol, I'll-"

"What? Have me arrested? Are you covering for her?"

"There's nothing to cover for. What in the hell, people? Have you all lost your minds? You're blaming an innocent person for the death of our friends. Now, I know it's hard to hear but there's a killer among us. And I mean one of us. Sasha is innocent in all of this, I can promise you that. We're scared, I get it. But that doesn't give us the right to point fingers at anyone we deem as different. You all should be ashamed of yourselves. Are you all so scared that you're willing to become monsters to feel a little bit safer? Jesus, that woman has a young daughter. They moved here to start a new life and didn't ask for any of this. Get a grip, everyone, or this fear will destroy this whole town."

Silence finally fell over the crowd. Harrison's hands shook as adrenaline rushed through his body. Never had he been so worked up during a town hall meeting before. There was nothing left of this town to recognize. Fear had changed it into something else entirely.

"We need to run the witch out of town" Mrs. Hazel cried out, to which several people stood up and cheered. Harrison shook his head in disappointment, realizing there was no way to get through to them. Sasha wasn't safe anymore. Harrison was well aware of that fact. There was no chance of talking the town down anymore. Something drastic had to be done.

"I have no choice then. Effective immediately, there will be a curfew in place. Everyone is to be in their homes no later than six in the evening and remain there. Anyone caught out of their homes after that time will be detained and questioned extensively. Do I make myself clear?"

No one responded. In fact, he doubted anyone heard him or even cared. One by one, people exited the town hall. Mrs. Hazel chanted, "Stop the witch" over and over as they went. Some looked at her in disgust but Harrison noticed too many had looked upon her in acceptance. There was no way around it now. For her safety, Harrison decided to stop by Sasha's home and see what he could do.

Chapter Fifteen

Sasha raced straight home after the town hall meeting. First thing she did was pack a bag of clothing and essentials. She intended to skip town, even if only for a few days. What had happened in the meeting had been terrible, frightening, and all-around embarrassing. The entire town was blaming her for murders she couldn't possibly have committed. To make matters worse, her affair with the sheriff had been exposed. There would be nothing but more trouble for her now.

"Tara, honey, pack whatever you can, OK? We have to leave for a while."

"But we just got here. Where are we going?"

"I don't know, sweetie. Just pack some things, OK?"

"OK."

Sasha hadn't thought about where they would go and with what money they would travel with. She had used every penny she had, and a lot of her mother's, to get here. There was nothing left. But that wasn't going to stop her. She'd sleep in the car if she had to. Of course, she hated putting Tara through such a thing but it was better than staying in Carlisle. It wouldn't be long before some nut job hurt her or Tara to "protect" the town.

"Hurry up, Tara. We have to go."

"I don't want to go."

"I know, sweetheart. We just need to leave for a little while, OK?"

"But why?"

"We just do. Now please, hurry."

But it was too late. She could hear the crazed mob forming outside of her home already. Before long, it would turn violent. They were screaming something and she couldn't quite figure it out for a few seconds. Then, she realized they were screaming for her to leave. *I'm trying,* she thought as she searched for her cell phone.

"What the hell?" She said to herself as she tore the living room apart. It was only last night she had used it. There was no chance it had vanished since then. Sasha was certain she had left it on the end table before rushing over to Sheriff Harrison's place.

It was a surreal moment for Sasha. Outside, a mob chanted for her to leave town while she scrambled around looking for a cell phone. In a less chaotic time, she might have seen the irony in the situation. There was nothing she wanted more than to disconnect from people and there she was looking for a device with the primary function to connect. But her mind was elsewhere and on more important things. Like the missing cell phone and- "The candle!" She yelled, surprising herself. She had remembered the candle. Like her phone, it, too, had gone missing. Someone must have broken in and stolen her cell phone as well. But why? A thought made her shudder. Someone didn't want her calling for help. It was all too much for her to take. Bursting into Tara's room, she took her daughter by the hand.

"We have to go right now."

Before she could lead her daughter outside, something large hit the front door. It sounded like someone had thrown a brick against it. Two more thudded loudly and Tara screamed. "Mommy, why are they throwing things?" Sasha couldn't reply.

All she could think about was leaving town to escape this utter nightmare. The town had turned rabid in a matter of hours. How was that even possible? She understood fear was a powerful emotion but these people seemed to have a heightened sense of it.

About the time tears started flowing down her cheeks, Sasha heard the familiar roar of Harrison's truck. Seconds later, he was out and pushing his way through the crowd. "Get the hell out of here, everyone. What's gotten into you?" He screamed as he made his way to the front door.

He didn't even bother to knock, he pushed open the door and stepped inside, making sure to lock it behind him. "You're lucky none of them tried that."

Sasha said nothing and wrapped her arms around him in a fearful embrace. There had never been a moment in her life where seeing a familiar face had brought so much relief and joy. Harrison wouldn't have all the answers she needed but it felt safer with him around. With the entire town ready to lynch her at any moment, his presence was a calming relief.

"I have to get out of here, Harrison. Your town's gone mad."

"I know. They're scared. You're the first major change to this town in over thirty years and it happens to coincide with the first murder in Carlisle. It's too easy for people to connect those dots. It will all go away once I catch this killer."

He cleared his throat.

"Which leads me to a question, actually."

"Can't it wait? If you haven't noticed, there's an angry mob out there ready to string me up. All they're missing are the torches and pitchforks."

"It can't. Do you have any reason to believe someone from your past is here to hurt you?"

Sasha's heart nearly stopped beating. What was he talking about? Did he mean her husband? That was impossible. He was dead. She had buried the body herself. There was no doubt in her mind her husband was dead.

"I hate to put it this way but did you owe money to the wrong people? Maybe your ex-husband did?"

"No," she snapped. "Why would you even think something like that?"

He looked nervous and ashamed. Sasha did her best not to be mad at him.

"Whoever is doing this seems hell-bent on targeting you. It's almost as if someone is trying to send you a message, not frame you."

"I'll tell you what's going on. Someone in this town doesn't want me here. They're willing to kill just to run me out of town. This has nothing to do with me. How dare you think it does."

"I'm sorry, Sasha. I had to ask."

Another brick landed against the front door and Harrison grew angry. As he turned towards the door, undoubtedly to give his town's people a piece of his mind, the distinct sound of glass shattering filled the air. They thought it had been one of the windows at first but Harrison realized something far worse had happened. Someone was breaking into his truck. He removed his pistol from its holster and flung the front door open. Before anyone could react, he put a single round into the bed of the truck. The group of angry townspeople who had been grabbing at any bits of the truck they could get their hands on, had backed off.

"This has gone on long enough people. Give it a rest. Is this what you all have come to? Breaking into my truck? I'm a God damned officer of the law and that's a felony. You people have lost your minds. I know we're all scared-"

"What the hell is this?" A man next to the truck cried out and held something above his head. Harrison's eyes took a moment to adjust and spotted the black candle. Even from where he stood, the name S-A-S-H-A in bold, carved letters was clearly visible.

"That's evidence from a crime scene. Put it back."

"Evidence?" A voice returned. "It was hidden in your truck. You're covering for her."

"Her name was found at the crime scene. She *is* guilty." Another voice cried.

"It doesn't make her guilty," Harrison pleaded. "I believe someone is trying to scare her. And right now, you all are. Please, everyone return to your homes so I can do my job."

But the crowd was no longer listening. Instead, they yelled and screamed and hurled insults at Harrison. "We demand she be arrested." A voice called out and Harrison ignored it. Sasha watched the whole thing from the window, making sure to remain unseen. The last thing she wanted was a rock to smash through the window and break her jaw.

Seeing the candle had nearly made her faint. Her name was carved on the side, clear as day. Harrison was right, it was a message for her. But who? And why? Her husband was out of the question. But maybe he had a friend or a connection that knew what she had done. Maybe they had come looking for her. Maybe the town was right. She might have brought this killer with her, albeit unknowingly. Though, she didn't think the town would care much about that.

Another voice broke the silence. It was one Sasha had not heard before, having narrowly missed her speech at the town hall meeting. Mrs. Hazel called out, "It's proof that she's studying the dark arts. Only a witch would use that candle."

Witch? What the hell? Sasha was beyond confused now. What kind of town, in modern America, believed in witches. Was everyone in Carlisle a complete lunatic or was she truly losing her mind?

"I'm not even going to dignify that with a response, Mrs. Hazel," Harrison said. But the old woman didn't give up so easily.

"You find demonic symbols on the body and black candles and you don't think it odd? The witch must have you under her spell."

"Mrs. Hazel, you've lost your mind. Why would her name be on the candle if she were the witch? Shouldn't someone else's name be on it for a curse or something like that? Jesus, I can't believe I'm even entertaining this farfetched idea."

Mrs. Hazel shook her head. "I don't know anything about black magic but that whore of a woman in there sure does."

"Hey, watch it."

"That's right, you slept with that woman. Maybe Mrs. Hazel's right, maybe you're under some sort of spell." An angry voice cried out.

"Get a fucking grip, people. There's no such thing as witches and there are no spells."

"Maybe she hypnotized you then." The same voice said. Harrison shook his head and rubbed his temples. This was only getting worse and he needed to put a stop to it fast. Sasha couldn't help herself from shaking, terrified of what the people of the town might do to her. They were accusing her of witchcraft now. It had escalated faster than she thought possible.

"That's what someone would say if they were being controlled." Mrs. Hazel said. Someone who had once been viewed by the town as "off her rocker" was now being idolized and followed blindly by countless people. It didn't matter what she was spewing was utter nonsense. The irony of the situation was palpable.

"Alright, I've had about as much of this as I can stand. Everyone disperses now or I'm going to start arresting people. You're going to go back to your homes and lock the doors. Everyone stays inside tonight. I'll keep Sasha at the station under supervision for her protection and to prove she's not guilty. I should be out on the streets tonight looking for a killer but you all have forced my hand. Instead, I'll be babysitting an innocent woman. I hope you all are happy. If another person dies tonight, the blood is on your hands. Go home and think about that. Now! Or you'll sleep in a cell."

He screamed the last sentence and the group started to break apart. Sasha sighed and dropped to her knees. Finally, it seemed as if something had gotten through to them. Maybe it was the threat of being arrested. Or, most likely, it was the promise of leaving Sasha locked up in a cage like an animal which had quenched their anger.

With the curtains completely closed, Sasha missed all the nasty looks which were flashed towards her house. People still distrusted her. Had she seen them, she might have still been worried. Who knew if one of these fanatics would come for her in the middle of the night to kill her. She hoped Harrison was being serious. Being locked in a cell all night sounded better than being beaten to death by the entire town.

Harrison remained outside to make sure there were no stragglers. When they were finally gone, he headed back inside.

Sasha threw her arms around him and held back tears. Nothing in her life had been as terrifying as this. She would elect to face her abusive husband a thousand times before being ambushed by an angry mob any day. With Brent, she knew what to expect. With these people, she had no clue.

"I think I better make good on my promise," he said. "For your sake and the towns."

Sasha nodded, happy he had been serious. When she pulled away from him, she saw a black candle in his hand. There was something carved into the wax but she couldn't quite make it out. Before she could ask Harrison about it, he held it up in front of her.

"Sasha, I have to ask. Do you have any clue about this?"

She could see the words clearly now. Her name, clear as day, had been etched into the side of a solid black candle. In fact, it was *the* solid black candle which had been stolen from her home. Ice raced through her veins and she thought she might faint. Nothing in her life had ever come close to the fear she was feeling now.

"What do you mean? You think I have something to do with this?"

"No, but I need to cover my bases here."

"What exactly are you asking me?"

"Do you have any reason to believe someone may have followed you into town and did all of this?"

"Of course not! Don't you think I would have told you if I thought I knew who it was?"

"I do. But maybe you don't know the person directly."

"Meaning?"

"Well, maybe your ex-husband had some bad gambling debts he never made good on. Or he had some enemies that might be looking for him."

An image of the freshly dug hole in the middle of the woods flashed into her mind.

"No, nothing like that at all. If he had enemies, I didn't know about them."

"This just seems too surreal. Why would someone here go to great lengths to scare you off? They're that afraid of an outsider they resort to this?"

"Why's that so hard to believe?"

"It's too well thought out."

"Thought out? A handful of random murders seems thought out to you?"

"These aren't random murders."

"What?"

"Come on, get your things together. I'll explain at the station."

Disappointed, Sasha ushered Tara to her room and told her to get her things together. She packed herself a bag as well. It was killing her, not knowing what Harrison meant by his last statement. These had to be random killings. Harrison had to be wrong. She could see nothing that linked them. Doing her best not to dwell, she packed her things and followed Harrison to his truck.

He had to wipe the shards of glass off her seat before letting her inside. The rioters had smashed the passenger window in order to get in. They're lucky Harrison hadn't shot any of them. She supposed it was the difference between a small town and big city cop. Back home, an officer would have shot a suspect for breaking into his car. But here, he knew everyone. He knew they weren't bad people, merely misguided.

Sasha envied him. He had the advantage of seeing these people as friends and family. He could remember the cookouts and barbecues. He could remember town hall meetings and holidays. When he saw these people, he saw a flock of scared people only wanting answers. Sasha could only see monsters.

The ride to the station seemed to drone on longer than it should have. The awkward silence between Harrison and Sasha seemed to be creating a tension that might snap like a spring at any moment. Sasha couldn't help but shake with anticipation. Finally, they pulled up to the police station and Harrison killed the engine. He sat still for a moment as if he were preparing to speak but then said nothing. Instead, he climbed out of his truck and helped his passengers inside.

"Of course, you won't be locked up like criminals. I'll have you sleep in a cell but more as a precaution and because there really isn't anywhere else to sleep" he explained. "Let me show you around before you sleep."

It wasn't an impressive building. It was mostly a wide-open space with a few smaller rooms built in. Clearly, it was not designed to hold a vast amount of people. Half a dozen people could fit in the cells, maybe. Even fewer officers would be able to work at once. Only a few brown desks sat in the center of the main room.

"I'll sleep here," Harrison said. "The holding cells are beyond this room which means no one gets to you without going through me."

"Do you really think someone will try?"

Harrison shook his head.

"It's the mob mentality. Everyone is scared and they're acting out at once. But no one person will try anything. Trust me, I know these people."

"How well? I mean, one of them is a killer, right?"

Harrison frowned. She almost felt bad for making the statement but decided she had meant it. Clearly, he didn't know his town as well as he thought he did. When he didn't say another word and led them on to the holding cells, she felt bad. It was clear he was upset. What wasn't clear was what he was upset about. It may have been the situation or it could have been Sasha's statement. She wasn't quite sure.

After opening a cell door with a key, he produced from his pocket, he said, "Your room, Madame." He forced a smile and she returned it with fake enthusiasm. Placing her bag down on the cot, she turned back to Harrison.

"Can you please explain what you meant earlier?" She was dying to know.

"Follow me to my desk."

She told Tara to stay in the cell and play with whatever toys she had brought for herself. Without any further delay, she followed closely behind Harrison to his desk. There, he sat down and put his feet up, offering her the chair next to him.

"Did you need something at your desk?"

"No. Just wanted to be comfortable."

She suppressed a moment of anger with him and sat down. Now he seemed to be toying with her and it wasn't right. There was too much at stake to turn the situation into a game. If he wasn't going to take things seriously, she would have to take matters into her own hands and flee town with Tara.

"All right, here's the deal. It seems random and at first, I thought it was too. I'll admit, the people killed are randomly chosen but there's a clear message here."

"And what is that?"

"You."

"Me?"

"Yes. The first death seemed entirely random, I guess most serial killings start out that way. It's impossible to pick up on a pattern or a signature with the first body. Unfortunately, the best way to catch a serial killer is for a few bodies to turn up. More bodies, more clues. But I'm getting off track here."

He cleared his throat.

"The first murder this town has ever seen shows up the same day you move in. Coincidence? Maybe. But the black candle left behind at the scene and the one stolen from your home is not. The Second body found behind your home and something left in your backyard for you to find; I like to think, once is a questionable, twice is coincidence, three times is a pattern. The third body is found with your name carved into another candle. I don't think I need to point out the obvious here."

"Ok, but what does any of it have to do with me?"

"Clearly, someone wants you out. It's a clear message to you. Leave town."

"Who would do something so horrible? Why not leave bags of shit on my doorstep like a normal asshole?"

"Here's the thing, I don't think it started out as merely a message for you to leave. I think someone was attempting to frame you. The third body seemed rushed, almost angry. The poor woman was beaten and raped before she was killed. Then your name was carved into a candle? Almost as if to say 'You're next'. Whoever is doing this lost their temper. The question is, why?"

Sasha's blood ran cold. Thoughts of her husband ran through her mind. But it couldn't be, he was dead. That she was sure of. No one could have survived the poison she had fed him. There had been no pulse. She had buried him. It was an impossibility.

"I gotta ask again, Sasha. Is there anyone who would want to hurt you?"

She shook her head and fought back the tears stinging behind her eyes. And it was the truth. She could think of no living person who would want to do her harm. The only person who ever hurt her was slowly decaying with a mouth full of maggots and worms in his veins.

"What about this witchcraft crap? Why leave black candles and upside-down crosses on the bodies?" She asked.

"Simple. Fear. Look what it's done to this town. They've lost their minds. None of them has ever been this close to a murder and there's a hint of the occult with it? They're panicking. Fear spreads like a plague. Even the most rational of people can catch it and do things they wouldn't normally do. One or two people would scoff at the idea of witchcraft but get a whole mob scared enough, well, they'll about believe anything. Mob mentality."

Harrison sat up at his desk and pressed a finger to his lips. He cocked his head to the side like a dog hearing the jingle of the leash. "Shit," he said as the dull roar of voices became clearer. As he stood up, he heard the sound of glass shattering. Pulling his pistol from its holster, he said, "You and Tara get in the cell. I'll handle this."

Fear coursed through her veins and she did as she was told. As she had feared, the mob mentality was winning.

Chapter Sixteen

"**Everyone, get** back to your homes now or I will start arresting people." Harrison could barely hear himself over the roar of the crowd. He knew the threat wouldn't deter anyone but he had to try. It was worlds above threatening to shoot anyone. It was the last thing he wanted to do, let alone threaten. The town was going through enough. They didn't need to be worried their sheriff would kill them too. However, things were escalating quickly in Carlisle and he barely recognized it anymore.

He heard screams from the crowd demanding he give up the witch. The looks of twisted anger and hatred on their faces was utterly terrifying. Harrison didn't want to admit it but he was scared. Nearly everyone in town had lost their minds and those who hadn't were keeping to themselves. Carlisle was seemingly changing forever. Sasha was going to leave town and Harrison was planning to go with her. There was nothing left for him here. The town he once loved was a shell of its former self. Paranoia and fear had ripped through the streets and nothing could ever be normal again.

More pressing issues were at hand, however. Once the angry mob had dispersed, he would load Sasha and Tara in his truck and drive until they hit the next town over. It sounded simple enough but Harrison knew it would be no easy task. The town was in a frenzy.

"Listen, everyone, I have Sasha and her daughter locked in a cell. She couldn't hurt anyone even if she wanted to."

"You'll just let her out." A voice cried out.

"Yeah, she has you under her spell." Another said.

"Jesus fucking Christ, listen to yourselves. Spells? Witches? Have you all gone mad? Did we take a step back in time to the god damned days of the Puritans?"

This did nothing to calm the crowd down. They screamed and yelled as loud as ever. Harrison could feel his patience slipping away from him. What was there left to do? Reasoning with them was out of the question. There seemed to be nothing left for him to do. His only idea would surely be a bust.

At that moment, another brick flew through the air and crashed against the wall to his left. His decision had been ultimately decided for him. Drawing his pistol, he pointed it at the crowd. There were a few gasps and most people quieted down.

"One more thing is thrown and I will shoot. Do you all understand?"

For a moment, he thought it had worked. Perhaps the mob would start to disperse. Instead, everyone in the crowd stood still, waiting for one another to make the next move. Finally, another brick sailed through the air, missing Harrison by mere inches. He tried to squeeze the trigger but found he couldn't. Instead, he turned and bolted back inside, locking the door behind him. The glass was smashed but it would buy him the precious seconds he knew he needed.

"Quick," he yelled as he turned the corner. "We need to get you out of the building." The sound of the front door bursting open echoed through the corridor. "Now!" he yelled.

Sasha pushed the door open and grabbed her daughter by the hand. Yanking her from the cell, they ran to Harrison's side. Without saying a word, Harrison led the duo towards a different room. He spotted the back door and darted towards it. The mob of people flooded behind them like a pack of zombies, hungry for flesh.

Harrison splintered the door open with his foot and pushed the two of them outside but the mob had already caught up. He was shoved violently over the threshold and toppled to the dirt below. Sasha and Tara were quickly surrounded.

Hands grabbed at them from all over, pulling their clothes and hair. When Tara began to cry, Harrison leapt to his feet and charged at the mob. He threw his weight into the crowd and managed to knock Sasha free. She turned to help Harrison free her daughter but Harrison pushed her away.

"Run!" He screamed. "I'll save Tara." Before Sasha could resist his command, several members of the mob charged at her. She had no choice but to flee. While she ran into the open air, Harrison jumped into the middle of the angry swarm and covered Tara with his body. People scratched, spit, kicked, and punched. Someone was going to die tonight if he didn't do something.

Once again removing his pistol from the holster, Harrison fired it into the air. Almost instantly the group scattered in a blind panic, eventually leaving a heaving Harrison alone with Tara. "Should have done that sooner," he muttered.

"Where'd my mommy go?" Tara asked, looking up at Harrison. He could see the sheer terror in her eyes.

"Don't worry, sweetheart. She's going to be fine. We'll find her." He grabbed her by the hand and led her to his truck. When she was safely buckled in the back seat, Harrison climbed behind the wheel and slammed the door.

• • • •

OUT OF breath and scared out of her mind, Sasha ran through the town. A few members of the mob still followed after her. After hearing the gunshots, some had vanished. It seemed a few were still determined. Breaking line of sight, she was able to hide behind a tree while her pursuers ran past. For two whole minutes, she remained perfectly still. There was a real fear they would double back and find her but she did her best not to think about it. There was no telling what they would do if they did. Her imagination ran wild.

Under the cover of darkness, she dared to leave her hiding spot. Everything seemed to be clear but looks could be deceptive. She knew that better than most. Playing it safe, Sasha crouched down low and kept herself out of view. She weaved through the streets of the small town, which now seemed more like a large prison.

She hardly cared about her own safety. Her thoughts were on nothing but finding her daughter and getting her out of this town. It was killing her not knowing what had happened to her and Harrison. She felt like a coward for running but there had been no choice. She trusted Harrison to do his best to protect her but he could have been easily overpowered. Sasha prayed someone was watching over her daughter.

Alone in the streets of this foreign town, she finally had a calm moment to think. Someone had worked hard to turn the town against her. But who could it be? She didn't know the town anywhere near as well as Harrison. There was little chance she would figure out who the killer was on her own.

Ducking behind a wall, Sasha checked the road ahead. Everything seemed clear. She waited another moment before moving out to the road. She wasn't entirely sure where she was headed but moving forward kept her relaxed. It was like having a goal, even if she didn't know what that goal was. Regrouping with her daughter was priority but she had to find safety first.

The sound of an engine in the distance sent a shiver of panic down her spine and she bolted to the side of the road. Hiding just beyond the tree line, she waited. To her dismay, Harrison's truck zoomed by before she could leap out and flag him down. However, she had noticed a small figure in the back seat and let out a sigh of relief. Tara was safe. Hopefully, he was taking her out of town.

Once her eyes had adjusted, Sasha recognized the road she was on. Up ahead would be a right turn which would lead her straight back to her home. It wasn't the best of options but at least she could find something useful like her cell phone. She hated not having the little device at the ready. She would be able to call Harrison and have him turn around to get her. Then they would all be on their way out of this wretched town.

Keeping in the shadow of the trees, she walked towards her home. A smell singed her nostrils and filled her lungs. She coughed for a moment but tried to stay silent. It smelled like burning wood and soot. The closer she came to home, the stronger it became. Of course, she feared the worst but curiosity kept her moving forward.

As she feared, she found her little cottage on fire. The flames licked towards the heavens with an almost hypnotic glow. But it wasn't the most disturbing scene in view. No, that title belonged to the mangled body draped in her front yard.

The blood-drenched body was nearly unrecognizable as a human and the head had been completely severed. When she spotted the decapitated head on the grass below, she nearly vomited. Upside down crosses had been carved on the cheeks and a solitary black candle lay only inches away. The wick burned peacefully.

Sasha had had enough. This town was full of psychopaths and killers. None of them was any better than the monster secretly roaming the streets. A terrible thought crossed her mind and chilled her to the bone. What if there was more than one killer? Maybe several townspeople had come together to share in the dirty work to run her away. It seemed possible. Hell, it seemed highly likely. The witch rumor would have been started by them, no doubt. The thought should have seemed a ridiculous one but considering the circumstances, she thought they sounded sane.

The fire would draw nearly everyone in town to her current location and she wanted to be nowhere near when it did. Hearing a car engine in the distance, she bolted past the burning house and into the woods behind. Once there, she found an area to hide which still gave her a clear line of sight. For some unknown reason, she wanted to know who would show up and what they would do. Curiosity had gripped her. Perhaps a little bit of fear as well.

It didn't take long for a posse to grow around the smoldering fire. Some averted their eyes at the grotesque scene in front of them. Others were merely enraged by it. A couple of brave men approached the mutilated remains and cut it free. Gently, they laid the body in the dirt and covered it with spare articles of clothing. Sasha would have found the whole scene sweet if the town wasn't full of bloodthirsty savages.

One of the men standing next to the body turned and faced the crowd. Sasha could only see the back of his head but his posture said enough. Clenched fists at his side, he began to speak.

"This has gone far enough," he yelled. The crowd clapped. "This woman thinks she can come into our town and kill us off one by one? Witch or not, this woman is going to pay for her sins. If Sheriff Harrison doesn't want to protect this town then it's up to us."

There was more cheering.

"We're going to split into groups and scour this town until she's found."

They began to break into groups of four or five and crowded around their new fearless leader like a pack of determined hyenas. Orders were barked out at each group concerning their search area. She saw one group point in the direction of the woods where she hid and she knew it was time to move. Her hiding place would only conceal her from the street. Surely, she would be spotted in a matter of seconds by anyone who entered the tree line.

As the group moved closer to the tree line, Sasha slowly crept away from her hiding place and moved deeper into the woods. Her heart raced and she desperately searched for a new place to hide. Every option she came up with seemed to be shot down by her own thoughts. Nothing was good enough and everything would get her caught.

Now, she found herself in the clearing where Tara had found the knife. It almost seemed poetic, being back where everything had started for her and her daughter. But there was no time to think about it. Instead, she found a fallen tree on the outskirts of the clearing and ducked behind it. It was impossible to tell in the darkness if she was completely concealed or not. The ultimate test would soon be upon her.

Less than thirty seconds later, the small group entered the clearing and walked slowly. Sasha could hear their feet crunch on the ground but did not dare peek over the log. It was nearly impossible to tell which direction they were headed. They seemed to be headed in every direction simultaneously.

"This is ridiculous." One of the female voices said. Before Sasha could rejoice about someone coming to their senses, she said, "She could be anywhere out here. How are we supposed to find her?"

"We don't have to find her, necessarily. If she's in here we might scare her out and directly into another patrol. Either way, she's going to get caught."

"Good point."

Sasha realized they were right. She couldn't just sit in this hiding spot the rest of the night. It would be too risky. Not to mention, her daughter was out there without her. Sheriff Harrison might have been with her but Tara needed her mother. A question now lingered in her mind, though. What if she did get moving and ran into another mob? What would she do? How would she defend herself? She had no weapons. She couldn't fight. What was she to do? A mob of four men would easily overpower her. Perhaps they would even outrun her. It began to make her wonder if running was pointless. Was she only delaying the inevitable? Maybe she was doomed to be caught by these insane people no matter what.

No, she couldn't believe that. She refused. There was a way out of this, there had to be. She had been through too much to let it all end in this ass backwards town full of paranoid lunatics. She had overpowered her abusive husband. If she could make it through that, she would survive this. However, the thought did not bring her comfort. Desperately, she tried to convince herself she would walk away from this but something deep inside her said this was how it all ended.

The little voice in her head which only pointed out the misery in life was back. It was a hard thing to fight under normal circumstances but now it was nearly impossible. Experts always talked about the flight or fight response in the human brain but they never seemed to mention how it worked in those who suffered from depression. Somehow, she had a feeling it affected her brain negatively.

The group continued through the clearing until Sasha could no longer hear their footfalls. Giving it two more minutes, counting each second out, she finally stood up from her hiding place. Her next move had to be into town. Without her cell phone, there was no calling for help. Her best bet would be to find an empty home, break-in, and use their phone. Of course, she didn't have Harrison's cell phone number but she hoped calling the police would do the trick. It was her only hope of getting her daughter back and getting the hell out of here.

Chapter Seventeen

Harrison drove around aimlessly looking for Sasha. His town no longer resembled home, rather, it seemed to depict a scene straight out of an apocalyptic movie. He spotted smoke billowing up towards the heavens in the distance and feared the worst. An eerie quiet had draped over the town and Harrison didn't like it. It felt too much like a benevolent calm before a violent storm.

Tara sat in the back of his truck kicking her legs impatiently. Harrison knew she wanted to be with her mom again. Desperately, he wanted to give that to her. Originally, he had planned to drive Tara straight out of town and come back for Sasha but his gut told him to find her first. There was no telling what the people of Carlisle might do when they caught her. The smoke in the distance made him wonder if they had already caught her. Images of Sasha tied to a pole on top a burning mound flashed through his mind and he couldn't control himself. He had to know it wasn't her. It seemed crazy to believe his town would resort to burning her alive like some sort of twisted witch trial but he had to be certain.

"Tara, honey, I need you to do me a favor, OK?"

"OK."

"I need you to sink down as low as you can in your seat. Think you can do that for me?"

"Yeah."

Tara sunk down in her seat giving Harrison a strange look. She couldn't understand Harrison was trying to protect her and he knew that. The less she knew about the situation the better. Tara becoming hysterical would not do either of them any favors. It was a miracle she wasn't already there, considering the torment she had already faced. Harrison found himself on edge. He couldn't imagine what was going through the young girl's mind.

Turning the truck around, Harrison decided to head towards the smoke. He hoped he would get lucky and stumble upon her wandering about. All he wanted was to reunite mother and daughter and get out of this town. Hell, he would probably never be coming back either.

No one in their right mind would come back after such a horrible display of violence and mistrust. The hysterical outbreak had damaged the peaceful community beyond repair. No matter the outcome of the night, Carlisle would never be like it once was. If Sasha would have him, he would like to move away with her and Tara. He'd grown rather fond of her. After all, she seemed like a strong woman. She had to be. Weathering this kind of storm and not falling to her knees in terror. Even Harrison was having a hard time keeping his composure.

Rounding the final corner in his truck, Harrison caught a glimpse of a horrific sight. Where Sasha's home once stood now had been reduced to a mere pile of embers glowing radiantly in the night. Loose articles of clothing were sprawled out across the lawn covering something thin and body shaped. Harrison's blood went ice cold. For the first time since before being deployed, Harrison prayed to God. *Please don't let it be Sasha,* he begged. *Please, God, don't let it be her.*

Before he could put the truck in park and check the body, an angry mob of citizens came bursting around the corner. They surrounded the truck and blocked his only route of escape. They banged on the glass and screamed at Harrison. A flurry of heads and hands burst through the open passenger side window. Harrison cursed, wishing he could get his hands on the asshole who had busted the window.

With no escape, Harrison reached for the only countermeasure he could. His pistol. Someone came climbing through the open window and reached towards the back seat. His fingers grazed Tara's knee. Tara pressed her hands against her ears and cried.

Like a hungry zombie begging for flesh, the man clawed and scraped at the back seat. Several others tried to pile in as well. No one heard Harrison's one and only warning over the roar of the crowd. So, Harrison pressed the gun against the intruder's temple. When it did nothing to slow him down, Harrison did the only thing he could do.

A small splatter of bloodshot from the open window, covering the faces of some now petrified onlookers. Everyone stopped moving and stared at Harrison. Harrison did not stare back. Nothing but survival for himself and the girl now mattered.

He grabbed the little girl by the wrist and yanked her from her seat. In one clean motion, they exited the truck. Harrison kept the pistol trained on the crowd, sweeping it from side to side. As they moved forward, everyone stepped back.

"Everyone stay back or I'll shoot again. I've had it with you psychotic freaks. Look at yourselves. There are bodies piling up in this town and every one of them is on your hands." He swung the pistol over the crowd as he spoke. Several ducked or shimmied to stay out of its path. He could see the fear in their faces and he liked it.

"I have seen some terrible things in my life but nothing as awful as this. You've all become monsters."

As expected, his words seemed to have little effect on the crowd. There was no going back now. Fear had won the day. There was only one goal for Harrison, now. Find Sasha. Nothing was going to get in his way. If he had to shoot every last citizen of Carlisle, he would.

“Who’s under the sheet?” He motioned towards the body with his gun. No one spoke up. “Please don’t make me ask again.” Still, no one spoke up. Harrison, naturally, feared the worst. The idea of checking under the sheet burned in his mind like a wildfire but he knew he couldn’t. Taking his eyes from the mob for even a moment could be a fatal mistake. He had to hope beyond hope it wasn’t Sasha.

“I’m going to take this little girl and get back in my truck. Anyone moves and I will shoot, understand?” There were a few mumbles and coughs but no one spoke.

Harrison pushed Tara towards the truck, making sure to keep himself between her and the crowd. If they rushed him, he would be able to push her out of harm's way. They moved towards the truck like an inchworm hiding from prey. All at once, as if the crowd shared a collective thought, everyone began to move. Sheriff Harrison was able to fire off one round before he was swept up in a sea of people. He gripped Tara’s hand as tight as he could but it was useless. They ripped the two of them apart and began to cheer.

Harrison was kicked, slapped, and punched as they dragged him towards the body still under the sheet. He could only assume they would kill him and bury the body next to Sasha. He was tossed through the air and landed with a hard thud next to the covered figure. Without hesitation, he peeled back the sheet and felt only an awful mix of emotion. Elation that Sasha was still alive but disgust that another citizen had been murdered. Who had done it this time? Had it been the same killer? Or did the mob collectively murder this woman?

"What have you done?" He asked the crowd. "You murderers decapitated an innocent woman. How could you? What did she have to do with any of this."

Finally, a voice broke the silence.

"Oh no, Sheriff, it wasn't us who killed her. It was that black magic practicing whore you sold your soul to. She killed her and strung the body up for us all to see." Carol Leighter stepped from the crowd and stared down at Harrison. She gave him a crooked smile and Harrison had to control the urge to knock all of her teeth out. If nothing else, the thought made him almost chuckle.

"Well, Carol, you've come a long way from gossip columns in the local paper."

"Me? You think I did any of this? I'm just a concerned citizen along with the rest of Carlisle. We deserve to be protected. We counted on the sheriff but he went and slept with the enemy."

"Sasha is not your enemy. She's just a woman looking to start a new life."

"And why is she starting that new life? Ever ask yourself that? She's a murderer, black magic or not. She brought death to this town and we have no choice but to stop it. The law is no longer protecting us."

"Jesus Christ, Carol, you've always been a pain in the ass but I always thought you were a sensible woman. I can't believe you would join this bandwagon of lunacy." Harrison spit a glob of blood into the dirt and a little splashed onto Carol's shoe. She ignored the gesture.

"The only lunacy here is the sheriff not doing his job." She knelt on her haunches and sunk low enough to whisper in his ear. "Is Sasha a witch? Probably not. Superstitious bullshit, most likely. But people are dying and it's clear who is behind it all."

"That's not how the legal system works, Carol. We have something called due process. Ever heard of it?"

Now Carol stood. "We also have the right to stand our ground, when necessary. And tonight," She paused for what Harrison could only assume was dramatic effect. "It's necessary. The killing won't stop until that woman is dead. You had your chance, Sheriff. Now, it's our turn."

With that, Carol turned and melted back into the crowd. Harrison desperately searched for her, hoping he could talk some sense into the mad woman but it was hopeless. She was nowhere to be found and the crowd had become riled up again. Now, Harrison looked for Tara. The sea of faces made it near impossible to pick out her small frame and young features but eventually, he did. She was unharmed but far from okay.

A hand gripped his shoulder and pulled him to his feet. He was shoved violently forward and decided against trying to ask any questions. It would most likely result in more harm. His captors, most of whom he had once called friends, clearly wanted him to walk. So, he did.

They walked for what felt like an hour. Eventually, they came upon a building Harrison knew all too well. It had been the focal point of too many town meetings as of late. There seemed to be no logical reason to be at the town hall but there they were.

He was forced down to his knees and watched as Carol stepped inside the building. A few others followed her inside and they began opening windows. Harrison's curiosity was close to getting the better of him but he kept his eyes fixated on Tara. She, too, was on her knees and tears rolled down her cheeks. If he hadn't been certain the town would beat him to death, he would have held her in his arms and told her everything would be alright. The poor girl had been through enough.

"Why don't you let the kid go?" Harrison pleaded to no avail. The crowd merely stood there while Carol and her goons opened every door and window in the town hall. Then, Harrison heard the familiar whine of the microphone and realized exactly what they were doing.

A loud *bang!* reverberated in his ears as Carol tapped the microphone. It was working loud and clear. With the volume at max, half the town would be able to hear every word she said. Before he could ask what she was up to, Carol walked out of the town hall with a death grip on the microphone.

"We don't want to hurt the girl." She said. An anger boiled up inside of Harrison.

"We just want you to give yourself up. There needs to be some form of justice brought for the sake of our town. You brought death and violence here. Give yourself up so we may have our closure."

She stood still like she was waiting for a reply. When none came she furrowed her brow and pressed the microphone to her lips. "You have one hour to give yourself up. After that, we seek retribution with the girl."

The microphone fell from her hands and she quietly approached Harrison. "You can't do this. You can't hurt that little girl. She's done nothing to you."

"Oh please, Sheriff. It's not us hurting the girl. It's her mother, the witch. The decision is hers now. Whatever happens next is on her head."

Chapter Eighteen

Sasha had been near enough to hear Carol's demands. Naturally, her first thought was to give herself up and spare her daughter's life. If she gave herself up, she would be killed. She knew that. But she also knew they wouldn't give up Tara, either. Giving herself up meant the death of her and her daughter.

She had to come up with a plan and she would most likely need Sheriff Harrison's help. She was incredibly outnumbered and completely unprepared. How could she take on an entire town? It was impossible. Ending her husband's life had seemed impossible but this was, by far, worse. If only she and Harrison had not become separated, maybe none of this would have happened. Though, she knew she couldn't dwell on what ifs. The fact was, Tara was in danger and she needed to do something about it.

Unfortunately, the only plans which came to mind involved poison. She had spent countless hours learning about different types of poison and what they did to the body. She knew how long it would take for a particular poison to kill a person and how agonizing their death might be. There wasn't a doubt in her mind she could poison again and get away clean. Hell, she thought she might be able to poison the whole town and walk away free. But it wouldn't do her any good. Unlike with Brent, she did not have the luxury of time.

Sasha decided she would move closer to the center of town and get a better look. The commotion was clearly coming from the town hall. The use of the speakers and microphone had given it away.

Moving between buildings, she crept silently towards her target. Once there, she saw a crowd of people gathered in front of the town hall. In front of the mob, on their knees, were Tara and Harrison. Sasha was filled with a pure rage as she thought about her sweet daughter being used as bait. It took every ounce of energy to hold herself back from marching into the crowd and clawing people's eyes out.

There were too many of them and she knew she could never separate Tara from them. Not in the current position they stood. Her only hope would be a diversion. The thought of luring the mob away crossed her mind. Then, she would be able to dash out and grab Tara. However, there would be no way to get away. They couldn't just run. Most likely they would be caught, assuming she wasn't caught while she went for Tara.

A simple, but seemingly effective, plan circled in her mind. If she could get her hands on a car, she might be able to get Harrison and Tara out to safety. She would still need a diversion to draw as much of the group away as possible. Then, she would simply drive out, get Harrison and Tara in the car, then drive straight out of town and never look back. It seemed simple but she thought it would work. If only she knew where to get a car.

If she could find one, she figured she would place it in neutral and push it until she was close enough. However, that would mean she would need to find a car with the keys already inside. Or, at the very least, finding the car keys in someone's home and then getting it back to the community center all in less than an hour. Seemed impossible. Sasha wished life was more like the movies. Then she would be able to hotwire a car and her plan would go off without a hitch, saving her daughter and her newly formed lover. They'd drive off into the sunrise and the credits would roll, insinuating a happily ever after ending. Reality was hardly ever so forgiving.

The harsh reality was far more uncertain. If they did survive this night, Tara would need years of therapy. She might even develop depression like her dear old mother. And Sasha would do no better. She too would need therapy, more so than she already had. This traumatic event would only help to break down whatever progress she may have made with her condition.

Then there was the sad fact of Sheriff Harrison. Sure, the two of them had shared an intimate moment but that did not guarantee a relationship. They hardly knew anything about each other. For all they knew, their personalities might not be compatible at all. Most likely, the two of them had been brought together by happenstance in light of tragic events. Happy endings never came in real life. At least, not for Sasha.

She realized it was no time for her pessimism to set in and did her best to shake it off. There was still a task at hand and she needed to complete it. For Tara's sake, she needed to make something work. She decided to take it one step at a time.

"First," she whispered to herself. "I need a diversion." She looked around her current surroundings, which was nothing more than a storefront a couple blocks away from the town hall. She thought about lighting the store on fire but had no clue where she would get the fuel to start one, much less a match or lighter.

No, her distraction had to be bigger. A fire could be put out. She needed something that would grab their attention and not let go. Something they couldn't ignore or easily deal with. She racked her brain but couldn't seem to come up with anything. Why couldn't she think of a plan? Her daughter was in danger and she was standing idly by without a single thought to save her. She had never felt more useless and stupid in her life.

As if to prove her wrong, an idea struck her. She was overthinking the situation, as she often did. The town was looking for her. The best distraction was, in fact, herself. Clearly, the town wanted to get their hands on her. They would use every resource available to hunt her down. If she were to make herself seen, they might leave Harrison and Tara less protected. Harrison would be smart enough to know an opening when he saw one. She was sure of it.

It was settled. She would use herself as a distraction to free her daughter. It was only fitting, after all. They had Tara because of Sasha so she had to make it right, even if that meant putting herself in danger.

Silently, yet quickly, she crept towards the town hall. It would only be a matter of time before someone spotted her. Though, she hoped to make her presence known by herself. Luckily, she received her wish. Crouching low behind a parked car in the street, she looked over the decent sized crowd. They murmured and shifted like they were awaiting orders from someone.

Before popping out, she made a mental note of which direction she would run. She didn't know the town all that well but she knew where her home was and the woods behind it.

She had hidden there once and she would do it again. That is if the town didn't catch her first.

Without a second further to delay, Sasha sprung from her hiding spot and yelled "Here I am you sons of bitches. Better grab me before I cast a spell over this entire town." After the words left her mouth and hung in the air, she immediately regretted them. Not because of how they would be misconstrued as a false admission of guilt but because of how corny it sounded, even to her own ears. Still, it had been said and now the entire mob had been alerted to her presence. She didn't stick around long enough to see or hear any reactions. Instead, she took off running at a full sprint in the opposite direction.

At first, she thought the plan had failed and no one would come after her. Several seconds went by before she heard the thundering sound of the mob in pursuit. She must have really caught them off guard. *I bet they weren't expecting me to pop out like that* she thought. The thought gave her a sense of pride and accomplishment. For once, she may have done something right.

• • • •

HARRISON PICKED up on Sasha's diversion right away. Clearly, the woman was using herself as bait to draw away as many as possible. That would make it easier for Harrison to free himself and the little girl. He respected Sasha's bravery but disapproved of her foolishness. Now, she was in direct danger and there was no way for him to help her. Now, he had no choice but to focus all of his attention on Tara.

Of course, that was what Sasha had wanted but Harrison was determined to save both their lives. He refused to let this town win. Carol had stayed behind as well as a handful of men and women. There would be no fighting his way out of this. He needed to stand up, grab Tara, and run. Then he would need to get to his truck. None of it mattered if he didn't choose the right moment to make his move. Too early and they would catch him. Too late and there might be no more opportunity to run.

He looked down at Tara and gave her a wink. The poor little girl was trembling. He couldn't blame her. He was scared himself. Pure terror must be pumping through her veins. It would be a hard road ahead for her, of that Harrison was sure. He could never have guessed how right he was.

Harrison reached out and grabbed Tara's hand tight in his own. When he felt the coast was clear, he stood up and bolted. Tara was pulled along behind him. "You've got to be kidding" he heard Carol yell from the community center. He took great pride in being a pain in her ass.

The remainder of the split mob now chased after Harrison but Carol stayed behind. Harrison didn't have time to wonder why. Instead, he dragged Tara in the direction of where he last saw his truck. With any luck, it would still be there and they would be home free. His thoughts turned to Sasha and he felt a pang of sorrow. They were going to catch her before he could get to her and he had no idea what they might do. He only knew it wouldn't be good.

Chapter Nineteen

Like a demented version of the running of the bulls, Sasha bolted through town with the mob close at her heels. She had managed to break line of sight a few times but they always caught back up. It was the biggest drawback of her plan. They all knew the town far better than she. But to Sasha, it didn't matter. Catch her or not, Tara would be safe. Of that, she was sure. Harrison was a capable man. She had not known him for long but she knew a good man when she met one. It took years of living with an abuser to develop that skill.

She choked on the smoke as she ran past the left-over remnants of her smoldering home. The safety of the forest was only a few yards before her now. The townspeople may have known the streets like the back of their hands but she knew her chances increased dramatically in the forest.

As soon as she broke the tree line she began to run in irregular patterns. Running straight would make it easier to follow. Instead, she snaked left for several yards, then straight, and left again. Eventually, even she didn't know which direction she was headed. *Let's see them follow me now,* she thought.

She could hear them crunching through the forest in a desperate attempt to find her. Tracking her would be difficult, sure. But Sasha realized they had the numbers to fan out and cover more ground. If they did, as they surely would, she would be caught. She needed a plan B.

There was no other option than up. She had to climb a tree and hide there. It was risky, sure, but it was the only option she had. Getting cut off would mean the end. At least up high she had a chance of not being seen.

As she continued through the woods, she kept her eyes open for the perfect tree. It needed to be tall with a lot of branches and a lot of cover. The darkness would be her ally. High enough and it would shroud her from those below.

Her lungs burned as she raced through the woods until she finally came upon a tree she felt she could use. It stretched high up into the heavens with branches that twisted and turned in all directions. The thick, green leaves would provide all the cover she needed.

Though her heart pounded in her chest and her mind screamed for her to move her ass, Sasha had to take a moment to breathe. She was winded. Climbing a tree in this condition and she would be likely to fall. On the positive side, it would be the fall that killed her and not the town.

It was now or never. The ever-approaching sound of the townspeople drew closer. Sasha reached for the lowest branch and gripped it with both hands. It took all of her strength to pull her legs up and wrap them around. Once secured, she was able to pull herself up on to the branch.

There was plenty of room for her to stand. She did so, reaching for the branch above her. Unfortunately, it was just out of her reach. There was no time to climb around the base and find another branch. The mob was almost upon her. Instead, she did the only thing she could think of and prayed it worked.

She leapt as high as she could and grasped at the branch wildly. Her arms wrapped around it but the bark scratched up her forearms. Ignoring the pain, she pulled herself up and took a deep breath. Accessing the damage, she realized she was bleeding. There was no time to nurse the wound, however, and she kept climbing. Luckily, she was able to reach the next branch with no issue.

Feeling like an expert now, she climbed several more branches until she was higher than she was comfortable with. Directly in front of her face was a bundle of leaves which almost camouflaged her totally from the ground. It was the best cover she could have hoped for.

Her muscles tensed around the branch as she lay her body down and gripped it with all four limbs. She could feel it sway up and down with her weight. Her mind conjured up images of the branch snapping and falling to her death, but not before taking a beating from every thick branch on the way down. But the branch would hold, she was certain of it. At least, she wanted to be certain about it.

She heard voices below her but couldn't quite see anyone in the darkness. They seemed to be staying in the area under her tree and she grew nervous. Had they seen her climb the tree? Were they figuring a way up? Then an even more sinister thought came to mind. What if they lit the tree on fire below her? There would be no escape and she would burn alive. She shuddered at the terrible thought.

Her fears dissipated when the voices below began to disappear into the distance. She wanted to hop down then and there but decided she should hide longer. After all, they hadn't seen her. It must have been a good spot. Sasha, however, was unaware someone had seen her climb the tree. Someone far worse than any of the townspeople. They simply watched the tree from the darkness and waited for her to come down.

• • • •

THE TRUCK stood against the backdrop of the night like a beacon of hope. Harrison knew what he had to do now. Sasha did not buy him time in order to save herself. She wanted Tara taken to safety and that's exactly what he was going to do.

He helped Tara into the backseat and tightened her seatbelt around her. With the way he intended to drive, she was going to need it. This town needed to be in his rearview mirror immediately. Of course, he couldn't help but feel a sting of guilt for leaving Sasha to whatever fate she might endure. Once Tara was safe, he would be back for her. But something told him it would be too late.

Harrison's foot touched the floor as he rammed his foot against the pedal. The tires squealed like a banshee as they headed straight for the town border. Luckily, the road was straight and empty. It allowed him to fly as fast as he could. Within no time, they would be in the next town.

A patch of standing water in the middle of the road caused the truck to jerk to the left and nearly fishtail. He was able to correct it before spinning out and decided to lower his speed a bit. If he killed them both in a fiery wreck, it would mean Sasha traded her life for nothing. If he couldn't save her, he would at least save her daughter. Though, he kept telling himself everything would be fine. He would be back in time to find Sasha and bring her to her daughter. His heart raced and it felt like every nerve in his body fired simultaneously.

Before he could do more to dwell on his thoughts, his cell phone began to ring. Forgetting where it was, he patted his pants pockets until he found it. Nearly dropping the buzzing device on the floor below, he pressed answer.

"Yeah?" He said with an inflection of impatience in his voice.

"Sheriff Harrison? It's Brian, from the lab. I've got your results from the prints you sent us. Thought you'd want that."

"Yes, please. What've you got?"

"It's kind of strange and doesn't make a whole lot of sense. I thought maybe it was a mistake but I was told to get you the info right away. You must have a few friends working for the FBI."

"This is time sensitive."

"Right, sorry. We have a print match for a Mr. Corey B. Hall."

"Who the hell is Corey Hall? I've never heard of the guy."

"He actually comes up as a missing person."

"Are you suggesting some random missing person showed up in my town and started killing people?"

"Looks that way, Sheriff."

That couldn't be possible. Harrison chose not to believe it. After all, why would he believe it? The killer had targeted Sasha. Why would a complete stranger to the town target another complete stranger? None of it made any sense.

"No, that can't be right."

"I'm reading you the results clear as day. According to this, Corey Hall is walking the streets of your town. Maybe you can track down his relatives and see what you can learn."

"Do you have a name of a closest relative?"

"In fact, I do. Hang on, I put them around here somewhere."

Harrison heard the technician shuffle through papers and grunt as he knocked something off of his desk. Finally, he found what he was looking for and congratulated himself with an audible clap and a snicker to himself.

"Alright, looks like he has a wife and daughter. Sasha and Tara Hall."

Harrison had to stop himself from slamming on the brake. It took every fiber of his being not to overreact and startle Tara in the backseat. His heart thudded wildly in his chest and he was certain his blood pressure had risen dramatically.

"Are you certain about this?"

"God damned positive," the technician said. Harrison thanked him for his time and hung up. It took nearly another mile for everything to settle in and Harrison realized he needed to go back. Sasha's husband was responsible. If Harrison could expose him, he'd save Sasha and stop the town from becoming the monster he already knew they were capable of being. Finding the man would be difficult but not impossible. It was a small town. He was bound to turn up somewhere. More amazingly was the fact no one had seen him thus far. Word spread quickly in the quiet little town of Carlisle, Maine.

Sheriff Harrison stomped on the brake pedal and spun the truck around. Headed back towards town, he pressed the accelerator as far as it would go. Time was no longer a commodity he could afford to waste. Corey would undoubtedly make his final move soon. Sasha was like a rat trapped in a maze. The closer she came to the cheese, the fewer chances she had for survival. But Harrison intended to increase her chances. In fact, he planned to raise them to one hundred percent.

Too many people had died. Far too much destruction had been caused. Harrison had been unable to stop any of it. He would be damned if that trend continued. He figured it would be with his dying breath he stopped this madness. Either way, it would all end. The town would stop its manic witch hunt, Sasha and Tara would be safe, and Corey Hall would be arrested or dead. Of course, he preferred the latter. Considering he had taken so many lives, Harrison didn't see the harm in killing Corey himse-

The truck smashed a dark figure in the center of the road, crushing in the front end severely. Something penetrated the windshield and pierced through Harrison's chest. The truck skidded down the road several more yards before coming to a stop; tires squealing on the pavement. Mangled bits of debris littered the grass and road about the area. Fluids leaked from the bottom of the truck and pooled in a dark circle. A crimson liquid ran from the grill of the truck where a large moose was embedded and pooled in the center of the road. Its antlers had gone through the windshield and struck Harrison square in the chest. He wriggled and pulled, trying to get free of the obliterated animal but it was no use. He was pinned to the seat behind him. Even worse, he could hear the wheezing sound of one lung desperately trying to keep inflated. Blood welled up in his mouth and poured into his neatly trimmed beard.

Through the pain and lack of functioning lungs, he was able to only utter one sentence. "Tara...are you...alright?" When he heard a faint *yes* come from the back seat and a quick check of the rearview mirror confirmed this, he allowed the darkness to take over his body and pull him down into the deep recess of death.

Chapter Twenty

Everyone had cleared out of the small patch of trees Sasha had climbed up. Once she felt it was safe, she climbed back down. A couple of times she lost her footing and nearly slipped off a branch. Luckily, she was able to catch herself before any real harm could be done. When her feet finally touched firm ground, she let out a sigh of relief. Anxiety shook her hands but she was relieved to have made it.

She was unable to revel in her accomplishment for long. She turned around to flee into the safety of the dark night but something seized her. A hand had shot out from the darkness and wrapped its long fingers around her throat and squeezed. She couldn't scream. She could hardly breathe. She kicked and scratched but nothing seemed to subdue the assailant.

Like a creature surfacing on a murky lake, a face came into view. It was a face she was all too familiar with. One that still haunted her dreams nearly every night. Her knees gave way. She would have collapsed to the ground if not for the grip around her neck from the man she had remembered burying in the woods.

The familiar face of her husband sneered back at her from the darkness only there was something different about it. It was twisted and distorted, like someone wearing an ill-fitted mask. Deep dark sockets had formed around his eyes giving them the appearance of retreating into his skull. His cheeks caved in grotesquely on both sides like they had collapsed in due to lack of a jaw. A theory which he confirmed when he gave her a toothless grin. Only, it wasn't just toothless. The entirety of his mouth looked brown and rotten like the inside of a bad apple.

"Take a good look." He sneered. "You did this to me."

"Me? How?"

"Turns out your little trick hadn't been enough to kill me." He spoke with a hiss from the many missing teeth. Spittle ejected from his mouth with each new word. The scene disgusted Sasha to the verge of vomiting.

"I...I... buried you. You were dead. This isn't possible."

"Yes, yes you did bury me. But I wasn't dead. I clawed my way out of that pile of dirt. I escaped death but not without a few scars." He pointed to his face and laughed. "Ironic, isn't it? Your past is literally back to haunt you. Tonight, I'm burying you in the woods but you're not coming back."

Sasha trembled in front of the man she had spent so much time trying to forget. He forced her to her knees and she considered begging for her life. She couldn't help but think about letting him have his way with her. Maybe it would buy her some time. Maybe he would let her live. She could only assume it was all part of his plan anyway. She was going to die right here.

"It's been you all this time, hasn't it?"

"I told you I would find you if you ever left me. I promised it would be far worse, didn't I? It worked out far better than I could have ever imagined. These inbred morons accused you of being a witch. I would have settled for murderer but witch? That's too good. They plan to burn you at the stake, you know? I might just hand you over to them. That is, after I'm finished with you."

Sasha should have felt fear. There should have been panic shutting down her will to fight. So many times, she had cowered in the corner while Brent viciously attacked her or had his way with her. Every instance had felt the same. Cowardice paved way for survival. This time, however, was different. Something felt different. There was no fear. There was no panic. All of it had been swept away in a single moment. She wondered if after everything which had happened to her tonight she had finally found a way to plant her feet and become immovable.

"No." She said, looking up at the vile man above her. Brent still clutched her throat but kept a loose grip. "I'm done being afraid of you. I'm done being afraid of everything. It's controlled too much of my life. If I die tonight then so be it. But I won't be dying a coward."

Brent scoffed, clearly amused. He loosened his grip on her throat a little more and reached down at her pants with his free hand. Sasha knew he meant to rip them off and take her here in the woods. She had decided it would not happen.

As the button came undone, her fingers searched the dirt for anything she could use. They slid across the rough and cool surface of a rock the size of a tennis ball. Digging her nails into the Earth, she scooped it free. While he pulled at her zipper, Sasha swung the rock toward his head. He never saw it coming. There was a tremendous *crack!* as the rock connected with his skull. Brent was sent toppling to the forest floor. For a moment, she thought she had killed him with a single blow.

His head lifted off the ground and extinguished the satisfaction Sasha had felt. A new dent had formed above his temple and blood poured from the wound and into his ear. Still clutching the rock, Sasha pounced on the man and swung it again but was unable to land another blow. He blocked her strike and threw her to the ground.

Brent was on top of her now, prying the rock from her fingers. She did her best to hold it tight but it was no use. The rock was ripped from her grasp and, to her surprise, flung deep into the trees. She had been certain he would have knocked several of her teeth out first.

He slid a finger down the side of his face, drenching it in blood. Before Sasha had time to react, he shoved it into her mouth. She felt his nasty finger against her tongue and on her teeth. He worked it into every corner of her mouth while she tried to pull away. Several times she tried to bite down but Brent kept a firm grasp on her jaw.

The moment his finger was removed from her mouth, she spit directly into his face. This only seemed to make the brute laugh. He wiped away the blood-filled mucus with one finger and clenched her throat again.

"Oh honey, you used to swallow." He bellowed a guttural laugh and began to unzip his pants. The moment had finally come. She was right back where it all started. He would rape her again and she would eventually submit. Her place would be at his feet like a wounded pup and she would lick his heel without question. He would use her and abuse her until he was finished and she would be left for dead in the woods. It was most certainly her fate.

But she refused. Death was fine by her but his rotten member would never enter her again. She would rip it off with her bare hands. Not a chance in hell would he be having his way with her tonight or ever again.

He leaned in closer and she could feel his stiffness against the crotch of her pants. "Just like old ti-" Sasha had pushed her head forward, baring her teeth. Then, she sank them into the soft flesh that was Brent's nose, like butter. Something crunched between her teeth and Brent screamed in a blind panic. Twisting her head back and forth like a dog with a chew toy, she attempted to rip it from his face. Instead, Brent was able to free himself and push her away. Falling back to the ground, he cupped his hands around his face.

His nose had split open and shreds of flesh hung freely on either side. Blood poured over his lip and dripped off his chin. There were tears in his eyes and he cried out in pain. Sasha knew it would be her only time to strike.

With little regard for her own safety, Sasha snatched up a nearby fallen tree branch and rushed at Brent. As she cracked it over his head, he toppled to the ground. No hesitation. She flung her body on him and struck several more times. Large pieces of the branch broke free and splintered into the darkness. The stick was reduced to a sharpened harpoon. It was like the universe begged her to take his life.

"You don't want to do this, Sasha." He begged for his life but did his best to hide behind his controlling demeanour. "You're not as cold-blooded as you think. The last attempt didn't work because you didn't want it to. Deep down you know you need me in your life. I complete you. Look what happened when you tried to make it on your own. The whole town is trying to kill you."

"Because of you! The whole town is accusing me of some black magic shit because of you!"

"I told you, that wasn't my intention."

"Oh yeah? And what were your intentions?"

"I admit," he mumbled through the blood still pouring over his lips. "My goal *was* to frame you for murder. At the very least, I wanted them to indirectly blame you for everything. I never thought they'd actually think you were a witch. It was just supposed to make you look crazy. It's incredible, isn't it? Who would have thought there would be puritan level paranoids in this modern age? I mean, shit. I wanted to get you locked up for murder. But burned at the stake? Now, that's poetic justice."

Sasha couldn't listen to any more of his bullshit. He had orchestrated the whole thing to make her look guilty from the start. He wanted to get her imprisoned or killed. Though she hated to admit it, his plan had gone off without a hitch. In fact, it went better than he could have planned. She knew there would be little chance she would survive the night. There was an army of people out there looking for her, even now. It was only a matter of time before she was caught. Maybe the town would come to their senses before they did anything irrational. But she knew better. Fear was like a virus. Once it spread, it was nearly impossible to stop. It took hold of this town and infected nearly everyone. The only cure was her inevitable death.

She looked down at Brent. From this angle, she wondered how she ever found him threatening. She could now see him for what he truly was. A coward of a man. He had always been a coward. Tears rolled down his cheeks, no doubt from the pain of his shredded nose. Blood stained his chin and neck and his chest heaved with the unmistakable spasm of fear.

"Do me a favor," Sasha said. "Stay dead this time, Corey."

“You know I hate that n-”

Before he could finish his sentence, Sasha brought the sharp end of the stick down and into his eye socket. It squished with a sickening sound and blood squirted from the wound. He screamed as Sasha turned the stick in circles, hopefully scrambling his brain. As she pulled the stick from his eye socket, the remainder of the eye came with it. Corey's head fell back and went limp. Unsure if he was alive or dead, Sasha plunged the stick under his chin and left it there. There was no doubt in her mind he was dead. This time, he would stay that way.

A wave of emotion struck her like a runaway bus and she collapsed into the dirt. Tears flooded over her cheeks. The blood on her hands disgusted her and she wanted nothing more than to wash it clean from her body. She would burn them with scalding water if she could stand it. She wished she could scrub her memory as well. Having to murder her husband had been difficult the first time around. Unfortunately, she had to commit the act twice.

As she wallowed in the dirt and cried, she heard the sound of footsteps approaching. Before she had time to look, she heard a voice cry out "I found the witch! She's killed again!" Sasha cursed as she pulled herself to her feet and bolted into the darkness.

Chapter Twenty-One

With ringing ears and a white-hot pain in her left arm, Tara stared into the darkness slowly encompassing her. Without the headlights, the world was utterly dark. The body of Sheriff Harrison was still pinned to the driver seat in front of her. It was a terrible reality for a girl of only nine to endure and yet it was all too real. She was all alone. The only person who could have helped her was now dead. Desperately, she wished her mother would arrive to pull her free from the car. She knew better, however. This was something she would have to do alone.

Her hands danced around in the dark, looking for the seat belt release. Giving it a press, her heart sank. It didn't budge. Panic set in and she tried to search for anything that would help set her free, though she had no clue what to do. Tears streamed down her face and she fought back the urge to scream out for her mother.

The man driving her around had been a police officer. Surely, he would have something to cut the belt free. Perhaps a knife? Reaching her hands into the darkness, she felt the seat in front of her. But when she leaned forward the seat belt stayed tight. There was no chance of reaching anything.

The panic hit her harder now. Tears erupted and rolled down her face in rushing waves. Violently, she kicked her legs like it would set her free. She did cry out for her mother, no longer thinking it would be useless. Fear was all she knew now.

After a few minutes, she was able to calm herself and an idea came to mind. *What if I squeeze out?* she thought. Tara figured she was small enough, it might work. Getting to work, she began to wiggle back and forth, pushing up with her legs. The seat belt was tight against her but she thought she felt it give a little. She tried this several more times before realizing she wasn't moving enough. Her legs were simply too weak to push her free. Tara needed more leverage.

Again, her hands shot around in the darkness for anything she could find. Her hand touched the cool glass next to her head and slid up. It landed on the grab handle and, suddenly, an idea was born. *I can use this to pull myself up,* she thought.

Tara grabbed the handle and pulled with all of her might, simultaneously pushing up with her legs. This time she moved more than an inch but the seat belt kept her pinned down. She realized pulling straight up would get her nowhere. Instead, she needed to pull at an angle. She put the shoulder strap behind her and tried again. This time, she shifted her body weight forward. It worked. The lap belt had slid from her waist and down to her thighs. There was no going back now.

Wrapping each hand around the headrest in front of her, Tara pulled with all of her might. The lap belt slid even further but seemed to be stuck at her knees. If she let go now, she would tumble to the floor and be stuck with the lap belt tight around her knees. Her arms burned as she gripped the headrest tighter. The lap belt scraped against her legs but she barely noticed. She centered all of her energy with her arms.

Reaching forward to gain more leverage, she bumped the lifeless body of Sheriff Harrison. Realizing she had touched a dead body, Tara nearly let go of the seat. She was crying now. Harrison's body slid forward and landed against the blinker. At first, she only heard the repeating click of the blinker as it flashed through the never-ending darkness. Her mind was so focused on pulling herself free, she didn't notice the figures approaching the truck. When she did, she could only see them in the flashing orange light of the blinker. The strobing blinker made it appear as if the figures weren't actually in motion but merely drifting through the darkness. The effect was eerie and made Tara scream in panic.

She hadn't meant to make a noise. She had wanted to remain still in the hopes the people would walk by. But now they knew she was there and they ran towards the disabled vehicle. In the orange blinking light, Tara thought they looked like a swarm of zombies ready to tear her limb from limb. With the last bit of strength her arms could muster, she pulled the headrest and shimmied her legs back and forth. Finally, they slipped free of the belt. Letting go of the headrest, she fell to the floor. Before she could escape out the side door, however, hands burst in through every open window available. It looked like something out of a nightmare. Hands protruded from the darkness, seemingly with no bodies. She crawled across the back seat to the other door but faces appeared in the window. Tara moved back to her own door but they were there too. She cried as the door was pulled open and she was dragged out into the night.

Chapter Twenty-Two

Her lungs felt like they would collapse at any minute. Sasha had lost her pursuers a while ago but kept running out of pure fear. This night had been the longest in her life and being separated from her daughter had only served to make it worse. She knew she had to leave town, even if she wasn't sure her daughter had made it out with Harrison. Her only problem now, she had no idea which way was which. Taking a random road could lead her right to her captors. She needed a way to gauge direction.

Far off in the distance, she spotted a tall water tower and she remembered Harrison showing it to her the night he drove her around. It seemed like weeks ago. If she could make it to the tower and get a bird's eye view, she might be able to make it out of this godforsaken town.

Trekking down the road, she made sure to stick close to cover in case she needed to hide. But the streets seemed unusually still. Sasha thought she would feel relieved but something told her it was bad news. Regardless, she carried on with her mission.

Surprisingly, she had no trouble getting to the water tower. Carlisle had become a ghost town in a matter of minutes. She shook her head as she gripped the cold steel ladder of the water tower. There was no time to think it over now. One rung at a time, Sasha climbed until she was at the top. The wind howled through her hair and she felt the odd sensation of gravity beckoning her to the ground below.

Trying to get her bearings, Sasha scanned everything she could see. From this height, she could see most of the town. She spotted the smoldering embers which had once been her home, if only for a brief time. She saw the town center, bustling with people. Before she could look away, she noticed something different. In front of the town center they had made a pile of something. If she had to guess, it looked like books and sticks. But that made absolutely no sense. Why would they pile sticks and books in the parking lot? Sasha knew she had to be missing something. She scanned the rest of the town before resting her eyes back on the town center, curiosity flaring.

Then, a rage burned inside of her when she realized something truly terrible. Among the disgusting citizens of Carlisle stood her daughter. They had found her. How? And where was Harrison? Had they found him too? Or maybe they already killed him? Sasha's mind buzzed with questions. She longed for a rifle. From her tower, she would pick off the vile people one by one. Killing almost seemed easier now.

A woman stood before the crowd and pulled Tara close. Sasha's hands involuntarily balled into fists and she pounded them against the railing. A voice came on the wind. Even with the amplification of the sound system, Sasha had to struggle to hear it.

"We...daughter. If you...again...give yourself...or we'll kill her."

The last few words had been eerily clear as if she had screamed them into the microphone. She couldn't be sure but she thought she heard the crowd cheer as she placed the microphone down. Sasha wondered how a whole town could cheer for the murder of an innocent girl. What kind of monsters must they be? Were they really awful or had fear driven them to this point? Sasha decided she didn't care. They were the enemy, plain and simple. She would get her daughter to safety, no matter what.

Sasha wasn't foolish. She knew giving herself up meant losing her life and that of her daughter's. But, seemingly, not giving in to their demands would get Tara killed all the same. It was a gamble she was not willing to take. But just handing herself over couldn't be her only play. There had to be something.

Desperately, she scanned the ground for anything she could use. She could only hope some sort of plan would formulate in her mind. Then, she saw it. She had to stop an evil grin from spreading across her face like a disease. Staring down at a parking lot, she saw several cars huddled together. It was perfect. Quickly, she began her descent.

Chapter Twenty-Three

Carol Leighter once again stood in front of her fellow citizens. The town she had called home was barely recognizable. Not because of the angry mob before her. Not even because of all the deaths. No, she did not recognize her town because it had let this evil become a part of it. Whether this Sasha woman was practicing black magic or not mattered little to her. In fact, she hardly believed it was real. However, she *knew* she had brought the evil upon this town, one way or another. There had been peace and understanding in Carlisle. Then, the bitch had arrived.

She had taken everything from them. Their innocence, gone. All of their joy, broken. Trust in those who swore to protect them, like Sheriff Harrison, dismantled. In the matter of a few nights, this disgusting woman tore the fabric of their quaint town apart. Carol loathed her for it.

Carol Leighter viewed herself as the savior of Carlisle. And why not? The sheriff had betrayed them and now he was gone. Her goal had been to merely run him out of town but the unlucky bastard had played chicken with a moose and lost. Perfect. The killer of all her fellow townspeople was being brought to justice. No more innocent lives would be lost. If it meant killing the woman and her little child, it would be worth it. After all, what were two lives versus hundreds? Carol would make that trade every time. In her mind, any reasonable person would. To not would be inhumane.

The make-shift altar before her had been made out of sticks, books, papers, and anything else which would be flammable. When the time was right, it would light up like a new year's celebration. Best of all, Sasha would find herself in the middle. A witch burned at the stake. The punishment couldn't be more appropriate. She felt like a puritan. They were the true saviors of this country, Carol thought. They did what was right. The women killed during the Salem witch trials had been the first step to cleansing this land of the impure. Carol knew those women hadn't sold their souls to the devil. But many of them were impure. Adultery, native sympathizers, and liars were all done away with. They only fouled up the land with their presence. Every last one of them deserved what they got. Carol was sure of that. Just as she was sure Sasha would too.

"No," Carol yelled. "Don't pour the fuel yet. It will evaporate before we're ready. We'll have to wait until we have the witch in custody."

Two men holding red canisters took a step back and placed them on the ground. Carol shook her head, wondering if she were the only educated person in the entire town. Sometimes she felt like it.

In the town hall, Tara sat with a bag over her head and a rope wrapped around her body. It led to the handrail leading up the stairs to the stage and held her securely in place. She wriggled around in discomfort and fear. Carol stepped over the threshold of the hall and approached the unsettled child. In one clean motion, she removed the bag from the girl's head. Carol saw the tears running down the little girl's face and decided to say something.

"Little girl, it's going to be OK." She lied. "This town merely wants justice. I know it's difficult to understand but your mother has done something terrible to us. One day, when you're older, you will understand what happened here tonight. When that day comes, you will want to thank us. We stopped a monster. You will see."

Tara looked up at the woman and wiped tears from her eyes. "You're the monster." She said with a leering glare. Carol held back laughter. The little girl had a fighting spirit. It would be a shame to kill her too but there was no other option. Even though they were doing the right thing, the rest of the world would call it vigilantism. In God's eyes, they would be victors but the world would condemn them. In order to keep the town safe, they would have to destroy all loose ends. God would understand, Carol was sure of it. She felt no remorse in her heart. Besides, her mother was a murderous, black magic dabbling whore. Who's to say her daughter wouldn't turn out the same. Killing the girl would prevent her from one day hurting others.

Carol placed the bag back over Tara's head and smiled. Everything was coming to an end. In a few hours, the town would be back to normal with this terrible incident behind them. Sure, wounds would need mending but like all great towns, they would come together to heal. She had nothing but faith in her happy little town.

She stepped out of the town hall and back into the night air. All around her, people sat and waited. Some continued to meddle with the stack of debris in the parking lot. Some only watched. Carol gritted her teeth. That bitch needed to be brought to justice before the whole town lost its nerve.

"She's out of time," Carol stated, grabbing the microphone once again. Her booming voice echoed through the quiet streets of Carlisle once again. "Sasha, your time is up. Your little girl will now pay-" A loud *bang!* erupted in the still night and somewhere off in the distance a fireball rose to the heavens. Simultaneously, a car came speeding down the road directly at the crowd. Panicked people ran in all directions to avoid becoming hood ornaments. In the pandemonium, Carol left the town hall door wide open and unguarded.

Chapter Twenty-Four

Sasha watched the chaos from around the corner from the town hall. She couldn't help but be proud of the plan she had concocted. Like something straight out of an action movie, the cars in the parking lot had been rigged to explode by ramming pieces of cloth into the gas tanks. She had found a hoody draped across the back seat of an older Mustang. After smashing the window, she tore sheets of the fabric free. Finding road flares in the driver side door in one of the trucks gave her the opportunity she needed. Leaving one car untouched, she found a rather heavy rock and placed it on the gas pedal. She also ran a long stick through the steering wheel, hoping it would keep it straight. Once all the bits of cloth had been lit, she started the car with the rock on the pedal and pulled the shifter to drive. It whined and revved loudly at first and she worried it wouldn't move but it did, tearing off at great speed down the road. A few moments later, utter chaos.

She now watched people run for their lives from the runaway car and couldn't help but smirk. There was no sympathy in her body for anyone left in town. One or two citizens of Carlisle nearly became nothing more than marks on the windshield. The explosions in the distance seemed to work perfectly. It caused the perfect amount of panic and chaos which she had used to sneak closer to the town hall.

When Carol had moved away from the open door, Sasha knew it was her opening. Sasha had fully anticipated fighting the old hag. She was confident she could win that fight but she would rather grab her daughter and run. They wouldn't stop until they reached the next town.

Sasha darted inside the town hall and spotted her daughter across the room. As she sprinted to her side, she could hear the pitiful crying from under the bag and it broke Sasha's heart. Quickly, she removed the bag and looked into her daughter's eyes. Immediately, they lit up with excitement and relief.

"I'm gonna get you out of here, sweetie." Sasha's tone, despite the chaos and excitement outside, was tender and loving. Her daughter had been through enough. There needed to be something to make life seem far more normal for her.

Without hesitation, Sasha untied the ropes and pulled her daughter to her feet. Before she could turn to run back out the front door, a voice called out from behind. Sasha's shoulders slumped in defeat. If Carol had found them, it was only a matter of time before others would join.

Sasha turned to face the older woman and shoved Tara behind her. "Let us go." It was less of a plea and more of a demand. To Sasha's dismay, the woman merely laughed. "We both leave your town and we never come back. Just let us walk out that door."

Shaking her head, Carol said, "I don't think so. Justice needs to be served. This town will never survive if the only murderer in history got away."

"That's what you don't understand. The killer didn't get away."

"You're right, she's standing right here."

"No, you're not listening. The real killer is dead. His body is in the woods. There's things you don't understand here."

"Let me guess, an ex-lover come to finish you off?"

Sasha nearly gasped at how accurate her description had been. For a brief moment, she wondered if the whole thing had been set up between Carol and her husband. But she quickly shook the feeling away.

"Well," Carol continued. "Maybe he killed those people, maybe you did it. Or you're practicing black magic. In the end, it doesn't matter. The town needs someone to blame and that someone has to be you."

"But I didn't fucking do it. I'm a victim too. Can't you see that?"

"You brought the murderer to us which means you brought death to this town. You're guilty either way."

"You're insane. I'll tell everyone out there the truth. They'll have to believe me. They will see *you* for what you are. A blood-thirsty, power-hungry hag."

Carol scrunched up her nose at the insult and a fiery anger burned in her eyes. Sasha wondered if the insult had been too much.

"And they'll see you as a witch. Which do you think is more terrifying?"

Sasha knew the woman was right. No matter what she said, the town would never believe her. Not as long as Carol had a voice. She would merely manipulate everything she said. It would end with her being punished for her husband's crimes. Worse, Tara would suffer for the sins of her father. Sasha would absolutely not allow it.

She turned to her daughter. "Run, Tara. Find the back door. Get out of here. I'll be right behind you." Sasha could hear Carol running up behind her now. There was no more time. "Run!" She screamed and pushed her daughter away. Carol lunged at Sasha but she kept her eyes fixated on her daughter. When she saw Tara had made it, she decided to turn her attention to the attacker pushing her to the floor. Sasha could only think of one thing in that moment. She didn't get the chance to say she loved her daughter one more time.

Kicking the despicable woman off of her, Sasha climbed to her feet. She grabbed Carol by the hair and swung her around with all of her might. Carol was flung on the stairs behind them. If Carol had been hurt, she was good at hiding it.

Carol stood up and leapt off of the stairs. She screamed as she did so, leaving an unsettling feeling in Sasha's gut. Like a bull chasing a matador, Carol charged at Sasha. Sasha sidestepped but not quickly enough. The two women flew into the seats in a tangle of limbs. Both women struggled back to their feet. Quickly, they were at it again. Punching, clawing, slapping, kicking. The two women wrestled for their lives.

With a sweep of the leg, Sasha brought Carol to the floor. She straddled on top and raised a fist in the air, ready to knock every single tooth from the woman's mouth. But several strong hands stopped her at the last moment. She was pulled off Carol and thrown to the ground. Several more hands pressed down and held her in place. She kicked and screamed and bit and clawed to no avail. They had won. They had captured her. Of course, she knew what this meant. Her thoughts turned back to her daughter. If Tara had made it to safety, it would all be worth it.

Carol, as if sensing Sasha's thoughts, approached her. "We're going to catch her, you know." She sneered as she adjusted her clothing and hair. Sasha could feel a dribble of blood running down her lip but she ignored it. Her mind raced faster than it ever had before. She desperately searched for a way to escape.

"Nothing to say to that, witch?" Carol continued.

Still, Sasha remained silent. It seemed to be eating Carol up inside and Sasha reveled in it.

"You're silent cause you know you've been beaten."

Nothing.

"Don't you want to plead for your life? Tell us you're innocent?"

Sasha smiled. Carol took a step back as if horrified but quickly gained her composure.

"If I were you, I'd wipe that smile off your face. Otherwise, the devil will do it for you when you get to hell."

Sasha's grin widened. "I know something you don't."

Chapter Twenty-Five

Tara ran. She ran for what felt like hours. She kept running until her lungs felt like they would explode. Then, she ran some more. When her body could no longer handle it, she collapsed on the pavement. Her mother had told her to run and she knew where she was supposed to go. It was far and she was tired. A quick rest couldn't do any harm. But the thought of the town catching her made her surrender the thought of a break and continued on, though at a much calmer pace.

She passed all the places she remembered seeing on the drive in. The road leading to the next town had to be the one she was on now. She was sure of it. Her little mind raced with anxious thoughts of saving her mother. If she made it to the next town in time, she could send the police back to save her.

For such a young girl, she had been thrust into an extreme situation. Most people double her age had never experienced such stress before. She didn't know it yet but it would take many years of therapy before she would ever be normal again. And even then, it would follow her for the rest of her life.

For now, Tara carried on her way towards the neighboring town. Hope filled her heart. All she had known, up until this moment in her life, had been her toys and her mother. She had barely known her own father before he had left them. This was the first real terror and the first misery she had truly felt. And it wouldn't be the last. Not by a long shot.

The town seemed to come to an end. The buildings melted away into nothing but endless forest on each side of the road. A few minutes later, she passed a metal sign that read, Welcome to Carlisle, Maine. Est. 1692 *Our Lands Whisper with the Echoes of the Past*. It was familiar. They had driven past it on the way in. She remembered reading the phrase on the way in and not understanding what it meant. Desperately, she tried to figure out its meaning as she walked. Tara needed something to occupy her mind otherwise terrifying thoughts would enter it.

The meaning of the sign seemed to melt away when she heard the call of an owl somewhere in the trees. The sound made her ears and curiosity perk up. It was a welcome sound in an otherwise awful night. Something about it was calming. Almost like knowing the world around her still went on helped take the fear away. She was too young to understand how her own mind worked. It craved stability and it found it in the nature around her.

She listened to the hooting of the owl for several minutes as she walked along the road. It was impossible to tell how long she had been walking but eventually, the hints of another town began to appear. Far down the road, she spotted another sign. It was too far to read but she could almost make out the word Welcome. She knew it had to be good news. Help was over the horizon.

Tara felt a new energy envelop her. Being within sight of a new town gave her the strength she needed to start running again. The welcome sign drew closer and closer as she ran. Tara panted hard but didn't give up. Flashes of her mother's face filled her mind. She knew her mom would never give up on her so she had to do the same.

When she reached the sign, she dropped to her knees and took in a breath. Her vision was blurry and there was a terrible ache in her side but she had made it. Finally, salvation had arrived. When her heart beat dropped to a normal level, she peered up at the sign and nearly burst into tears. Welcome to Eagle Lake. 5 Miles ahead.

Tara didn't know exactly how far five miles was but it seemed longer than she could walk. She pictured it taking all night and not getting the police until the next morning. By then, it could be too late. But going back wouldn't do any good either. They would merely hurt her along with her mother. Maybe, she could get there fast enough if she sprinted in small bursts. Or, perhaps she would get lucky and a car would drive by. She had seen many movies where people hitchhiked. All it took was a motion of the thumb. Someone would pick her up for sure. Determined to rescue her mother, little Tara started off again.

Chapter Twenty-Six

Strong hands pushed her along the narrow path to the center of the crowd. All around her, people hissed and booed. It was all strange and foreign, like something straight out of The Twilight Zone. The people had gone mad. She hoped beyond hope her story would have a happy ending, though something told her it wouldn't.

In the center of the crowd, she spotted the piled debris. Sticks, paper, books, and other flammables sat in a large pile. A tall, metal pole protruded from the center. She thought of pleading and fighting and running. But what was the use? They had the numbers. It would only be a matter of seconds before they forced her back into place. Besides, keeping the attention on herself meant Tara would have plenty of time to get away.

Her life had changed dramatically in only a few days. Where she used to feel broken and ashamed, she was now empowered. For the first time in years, she didn't care about her depression. Finally, she no longer saw herself as damaged. True, things were dismal. But, she had confronted her husband and finally ended that torture once and for all. She had saved the life of her daughter. And she had been able to put herself out there and partake in a romantic relationship. She had to take the wins, no matter how small. She would refuse to let this condition consume her like the hatred and paranoia of the small town of Carlisle.

She was brought to a halt in front of the pile and turned to face the crowd. Behind her, Carol Leighter climbed up on the debris and the crowd went quiet. She let the silence sink in for a few minutes before speaking.

"Before you all stands the woman accused of the most heinous crimes this town has ever seen. Murder and the practice of dark magic."

The town booed again.

"We need to bring justice back to our society. Those meant to protect us were swayed by the seductive power of this witch. He's dead now. God always prevails."

The crowd cheered and Sasha's heart sank. Harrison was dead? She wanted to know how. If the town had killed him, then there was certainly no chance of survival for herself. They had turned on their own. As an outsider, she was doomed.

"What did you do?" She demanded.

Carol laughed and looked at her.

"Not me, not us."

It did nothing to answer Sasha's question but she assumed it would be the most she would get out of her. These murdering bastards had killed the sheriff and now they would kill her too. But, Sasha knew, she would have the last laugh.

Carol marched her up on the pile, pressed her back against the metal pole, and tied her to it. It was at this moment Sasha truly realized the end of her life was coming. Sheriff Harrison was no longer alive to save her and her daughter could take hours to get help. This would be her end.

It would be a lie to say she wasn't afraid. However, something inside her felt unusually calm. Even in the face of certain death, she seemed to be handling it all well. Sasha did not understand how. Though she felt an eerie calm, survival was still on her mind.

"Please, let me go." She said, matter-of-factly. Her tone was void of nearly any emotion, startling even herself. "I didn't kill those people. The man responsible is dead in the woods. I've done nothing. You can't kill an innocent woman."

The crowd murmured and shifted uneasily. Sasha could tell some of them were beginning to have second thoughts. She realized, she wouldn't have to convince everyone, merely a few. If some in town were willing to argue on her behalf, it might convince the others the idea of burning her alive was crazy.

"He was my ex-husband. He was an abusive drunk and one night I took my daughter and left," she lied. "I didn't think he would ever find me but he did. He's the one who murdered your friends. Not me. Clearly, he wanted to turn you all against me. It worked, brilliantly. Don't be fooled by him. If anyone here is the devil, it was that man."

She saw some faces in the mob grow sympathetic and understanding. Others remained stoic. This was the moment of truth. If she were to change any hearts and minds, it would be in this moment. Her life was in her own hands. No one would be coming for her.

"I'm begging you. Don't do this. I have a little girl out there by herself. She's scared and alone. Tara needs her mother. There's no one left for her. I'm all she has."

That was it, she knew it. The last few words would save her life. Already, she could see people in the audience coming out of whatever fear driven trance had ensnared them. Now, she saw all of them for what they truly were. A community of sheltered individuals who had never experienced pure tragedy in their lives. Sasha actually pitied them. They weren't evil. They were lost and misguided. She knew better than most what fear could do.

"No!" A scream from the bottom of the pile pierced the air. Carol Leighter stood there with a torch and lighter. She pointed the unlit torch at Sasha and sneered. "She must be punished for her crimes. Don't let this witch cast her spell on you. She is deceiving you all, just as she did our sheriff. Her ex-husband was probably another pawn of her black magic. Don't fall for the lies of a wicked woman who sold her soul to the devil."

Looks changed from sympathetic to angry, though not all of them. Clearly, those who wanted to let her go were the minority. There would be little chance of talking the rest of the group down. There was only one other option Sasha had and she had been hoping to not have to use it.

Carol held up the lit torch and motioned to throw it. The majority of the crowd cheered. Sasha let out one more scream for attention and nearly fainted when it worked. A dead silence fell over the crowd. All eyes were glued on the woman on the pile. The next words from her mouth were risky and she hardly wanted to say them but it was all she had left. "You all need to let me go," she started. "If you don't, I shall curse this town and everyone in it."

The flaming torch danced in the night as she spoke. Sasha could hear it crackle as she took a breath. "Test me, and you all shall die an unnatural and terrible death. Do not test my powers." Her voice was deep and menacing, scaring even herself. Some stared at her in bewilderment. Others merely shifted their eyes away. Carol, however, stood strong.

"Do not fear the ramblings of a condemned soul. No curse can live after the witch is dead."

Some of the town's folk had been convinced. Whether it had been the fear of a curse or common sense finally kicking in, Sasha could not know. Several members of the crowd stepped forward in an attempt to stop Carol from tossing the torch and lighting Sasha ablaze. There was a feeling of relief unlike any Sasha had felt before. To her horror, however, it was too late. Carol heaved the torch onto the pile and it lit almost instantly.

The heat was intense and immediate. At first, the flames only licked at her heels. Sasha tried desperately to kick herself away from the heat to no avail. Some townspeople ran to her aid, looking for a way to extinguish the flames. It was no use. The fire was too hot and too high.

Carol raised her hands with the rising flames as if she could control them. Someone in town tackled her to the ground, clearly misunderstanding what was happening. Sasha's pants melted to her skin and she felt a heat, unlike anything she had ever experienced. Before long, the flames had spread to her torso and singed at the strands of hair dangling above her shoulders. Shortly after, they too caught.

Sasha let out an ear-piercing scream as the flames consumed her head. The smell of burning hair and flesh was pungent, though Sasha could no longer smell anything. From the ground, Carol averted her eyes as the thrashing body of Sasha burned and charred to a crisp. Her screams finally came to an end as the fire consumed her completely. The last thought she ever had was of her daughter, and hoping she had found safety. For Sasha, the pain and torture were finally over. But, for the town of Carlisle, it had just begun.

Chapter Twenty-Seven

It was well into the following morning when Tara found herself in the backseat of a police cruiser heading off down the road. She had wandered for hours the night before and barely reached the police station before passing out. Exhaustion had finally got the better of her. When she awoke, she was in the police station. A nice man in a uniform looked at her with a smile, handing her a bottle of water.

"By the looks of those shoes, I'd say you walked all night." Tara paid little attention.

"I need help. My mom is in trouble."

"Oh? Where's she at?"

"A different town." She pointed over her shoulder, hoping it was the correct direction. She had no clue which way the town she had come from was. There was little chance she would be able to tell from outside either.

"Closest town is Carlisle. Is that where your mother is?"

Tara thought about it for a moment. The sign she had seen as they drove in had said something about the past. She closed her eyes tight and did her best to picture it. The world Carlisle materialized in her mind's eye. Finally, she nodded.

"What kind of trouble is she in?" The officer pulled out a small notebook and prepared to write notes.

"There's no time. The town is trying to hurt her."

"The whole town? Did something happen?"

Tara shrugged. She didn't really understand why the town was trying to hurt her mother, she only understood they *were*.

There had been talk of murders but she knew her mother had nothing to do with them.

"Please, we have to hurry."

"Alright, let's take a drive down there and see if we can't figure out what's going on, OK?"

Tara nodded.

Once they were in the police cruiser and headed down the road, Tara wished they would go faster. She had already let her mother down once. She couldn't bear to be away from her any longer. Her foot nervously tapped and she stared out the window. The familiar sign of Carlisle zipped past and she knew it would only be a matter of minutes before they arrived.

The officer was immediately drawn to a group of people gathered around a large pile of ashes. Slowing to a stop, he rolled down the window and called for someone's attention. An older woman walked over with a somber expression on her face. Tara recognized her right away.

"What happened here?" The officer asked.

"A house burned down in the middle of the night."

"Everyone OK?"

The woman hung her head.

"Unfortunately, no. Someone was killed."

"Sorry to hear that. Where's the sheriff? Harrison, right?"

"He was killed last night. A car accident while racing to the scene of the fire. He was a brave man."

"Jesus Christ, that's awful."

"What can we do for you, officer?"

"I have a little girl here," he pointed over his shoulder. "She said her mom was here and she was in trouble. Know anything about it?"

The woman peeked through the back window and gave Tara a smile. Tara sunk down in her chair, terrified of the woman she knew as Carol. She had been the last person Tara saw her mother with. If something had happened to her, it was because of her.

Carol pulled away from the window and looked back at the officer. "Sorry," she said. "Never seen her before in my life."

Tara started to cry. The woman was lying but there was nothing she could do. The officer thanked her for her time and started to drive away. After getting back to the station, he sat her down at his desk and calmed her down.

"Look, honey. It's a pretty big area around here. Maybe you're thinking of the wrong town."

Tara shook her head.

"Well, we'll get an official investigation going and see if we can find out what happened to your mother, OK?"

Tara wiped tears from her eyes and nodded. But she knew it wouldn't be okay. Deep down in her heart, she could feel her mother was gone. The evil woman who had lied to the officer had killed her mom. A feeling of pure hatred coursed through her veins.

"In the meantime, do you have any relatives you can stay with?"

Tara told the man about her grandmother and he went about looking her up and getting an address and phone number. Within the hour, the police officer was driving her towards her grandmother's house. Every mile they traveled, Tara felt farther from her mother. She wanted to hug her again. She wanted to hear her voice. Knowing she never would again tore her up inside. She would never truly be the same.

Her grandmother took her in with open arms. The officer did his best to explain the situation, though he wasn't quite sure what it was. "There's an ongoing investigation to find your daughter, ma'am." He said. "If anything turns up you'll be the first to know." She had nodded and watched the officer walk back to his car.

Tara told her grandmother everything she could remember. How the town had turned against them and wanted to hurt her. Of course, she had told the same story to the police but they seemed to think it was merely a story developed by a confused child. Tara knew different. Something awful had happened in Carlisle and justice might not ever prevail.

Chapter Twenty-Eight

"I **'m telling** you, something was off." Officer Brown stated to his partner. "The little girl was really frightened. I can't believe she would make the whole story up."

"Well," his partner started. "A kid's imagination can really run wild when faced with hard realities. Her mother dumped her in the middle of nowhere and took off. It's been well over a week and no one has seen or heard a thing? It makes no sense."

Officer Brown shrugged but couldn't let the matter go. He remembered the looks on the faces of the people of Carlisle. It had seemed more than mere sorrow. He thought he had seen guilty looks among them. Many had averted their eyes.

"The girl said she was with Sheriff Harrison when he crashed his truck. She told me the people pulled her out and tried to hurt her."

"She was probably scared and not thinking clearly. They were trying to help her and she thought they were trying to hurt her."

"But that woman said she had never seen her before. How could that be if they pulled her from the wreck? Wouldn't she remember that?"

"Maybe she wasn't there."

"Tara was clear she had been."

"I think you're focusing too much on what the little girl said. Her story can't be trusted. Two major traumatic experiences around the same time have her confused. You're overthinking it."

Officer Brown started to wonder if his partner was right. After all, it did make sense. Tara had been through a lot. Her mother was missing and she had nearly died in a car accident. The accident alone would have been enough to mix up her thoughts. But the two experiences together may have impacted her more than Brown thought. Still, he couldn't shake the odd feeling about the town. His gut feeling told him to not let it go.

"Come on, Elton." He said to his partner. "Let's take a drive to Carlisle. At least put my mind at ease."

"Whatever will shut you up," Elton said.

The two of them laughed and headed out for Carlisle. Neither said a word for the entire drive. Brown continued to brood over Tara's story, knowing it had to be more truth than fantasy. He knew his partner did not feel the same. Something told him Elton would believe him before the night was over.

They passed the familiar sign welcoming them to Carlisle. Up ahead, things seemed unusually dark. Instinctively, officer Brown let off the gas. The street lights weren't on and no lights came from the end of the road where the town would have been. It seemed rather unusual.

The patrol car came to a stop out front of the town center. Its headlights bathed the front of the building in a white glow from the LED headlights. The entire scene looked like something out of an apocalypse movie. The town was just quiet and empty. Officer Brown shifted into park and stared out the windshield.

"Alright, Jon," Elton said. "I'll admit it. This is weird. Power's out and no one seems to be here."

"Yeah."

It was all Officer Brown could think to say. Too many thoughts raced through his mind. There was definitely something wrong. He opened his door and stepped out into the silent night air. His partner, Elton, stayed in the car for a moment, not sure what to think. Finally, he stepped out and followed his partner.

There seemed to be nothing in the immediate area that indicated trouble. Officer Brown pulled out his cell phone and switched on the flashlight app. Walking towards the town center, he noticed something off. The parking area in front of the building had several marks. He got down on one knee to take a closer look. Brown wiped at the mark with a finger. The black residue spread under his finger and stuck under his nail.

He sniffed the substance and shook his head. "Soot."

"There was a fire that night, remember? You said one of the houses burned down."

"Yes, but across town. Not here."

"Maybe they brought some of the pieces here?"

"Seems like a long way to transport garbage."

Brown walked towards the town hall and peered into the window. It was too dark inside to see anything so he sidestepped to the door. Finding it unlocked, he let himself inside. He held the cell phone out in front of him and swept the light across the room. The open space looked like an auditorium. Wooden stadium seats lined the floor facing a stage. He noticed something in the center of the stage and shifted his focus there. Outside, his partner scanned the road for any signs of life.

"There's someone in here, I think," Brown said. Elton didn't respond. Instead, he walked inside and pulled out his cell phone. Much like Jon, he scanned the auditorium with his cell phone. In the distance, Jon was approaching the stage. His cellphone pointed down at the floor.

"Ma'am, are you OK?" Officer Jon Brown called out, receiving no response. Now he was sure it was a person. An older woman lay in the center of the stage with her head facing away. A microphone lay a few feet away from her. "Excuse me," he said as he climbed up on the stage. He approached slowly, not sure what to expect.

Bending down, Officer Jon Brown reached out and rocked the woman's shoulder. It barely moved and he knew exactly what it meant. Rigor mortis had set in. The poor woman was dead. Wondering if it were the little girl's mother, Brown stood up and stepped over the body.

"Oh fuck." It was the woman he had talked to the night he had found Tara. She had leaned in the window and said she didn't recognize her. Now, she lay on the stage in a dead heap. But it wasn't merely a dead body that had made Brown feel uneasy. No, he had seen several dead bodies in his time. It came with the job. But he had never seen one quite like this. The poor woman had clearly suffered.

Her eyes were bulging from her skull like she had seen some terrible nightmare in her last moments of life. A mixture of drool, blood, and vomit covered her face and chest. Nearby stood a small, dry puddle of the same substance. Her teeth were loose in her mouth but not because she wore dentures. Her actual teeth had come loose. Scratch marks littered the floor like she had dug her nails into it to find relief. Brown also found blood and splinters under her nails. The most disturbing sight, however, was her tongue. It was swollen and caught in her throat. Her mouth was gaping wide as if to show off the horrid sight.

"Elton, we have a body here. Looks like this woman really suffered."

"Um," His partner stammered. "We have a lot more than just one body."

Officer Brown turned to face his partner. Before he could ask what he had meant, he saw the sea of bodies sitting in the stadium chairs. He had missed them all. The body on the stage had diverted his attention enough to pass every single citizen in Carlisle. Each had the same horror-stricken expression glued to their faces. Drool, blood, and vomit caked every single face in the crowd.

"What...in...the...unholy...fuck?" Brown stepped down off the stage and scanned the audience with his phone. "I've never seen anything like this before." Some of the citizens held hands, forever bonding their deceased bodies. Many held rosary beads and bibles. But the worst was the women, clutching their children. It was a scene Brown would never forget until his dying day.

"We have to call this in," Brown said. Elton nodded and dialed a few numbers on his phone. A few hours later, the FBI crawled over the city of Carlisle. Bodies were bagged, evidence was taken, and photos were snapped. Meanwhile, Elton and Jon stood by their cruiser and watched the controlled chaos. Both men had already given their statements.

"We found a lot of cars a few blocks away with all their batteries missing. Not sure what to make of that."

Jon shrugged. The FBI agent walked away and continued to converse with the other agents. As they did, Jon looked up the street and spotted the water tower looming over the town. It stood over like a dark tower in the sky. He stared at it for several long minutes before realizing something.

"Holy shit." He said aloud.

"What?" His partner asked.

"There." Officer Jon Brown pointed at the water tower. "They'll find their missing car batteries in there. I'd bet my career on it."

"Who would have done something so disturbing like that?"

Jon waved his hands and flagged down the agent in charge. "Hey, we need to comb this town for a body. A woman by the name of Sasha Hall. I think the people of Carlisle murdered her."

Acknowledgments

First and foremost, let me thank *you* for picking up this book and reading it. I wouldn't be able to do what I do if not for the readers. So, sincerely, thank you. I hope you enjoyed this book and if you did, please tell your friends and consider leaving a review on your favorite reading platform or on Goodreads. It's the best way to promote your favorite authors.

Next, I'd like to thank Roxie Prince who has been a patron of mine over on Patreon for about a year now. Your support has been super helpful, and I always appreciate it. Even just having someone to read the short stories or flash fiction pieces I write. Roxie has also been a great supporter of mine over on Instagram and an even better friend. Thanks for sticking around with me!

Also, I have to thank my new editor and friend, Nicole Cucci. Your help in making this book a reality has been detrimental and I'm not exaggerating when I say I couldn't have done it without you. Thanks for everything you've done from helping me edit to helping me name characters. You're the best!

Thanks to my wife for putting up with me shutting myself away for hours at a time and thinking about this story for days on end. It's not easy being the wife of an author, I imagine. So thank you for your support and belief in me.

Cover design by James, GoOnWrite.com

Don't miss out!

Visit the website below and you can sign up to receive emails whenever Evan Bond publishes a new book. There's no charge and no obligation.

https://books2read.com/r/B-A-ZJVF-XLKW

BOOKS 2 READ

Connecting independent readers to independent writers.

Also by Evan Bond

Ethan McCormick Series
To the Wolves
Sins of the Mother

The After Death Series
After Death

Standalone
Death Can Wait
Getaway
Echoes of the Past
Charred Remains

Watch for more at https://www.evanbondauthor.com/.

About the Author

Evan Bond is a thriller/suspense author who loves blending his love of the outdoors with his writings. He is the author of the best selling psychological thriller *Echoes of the Past* and his intense action-packed survival account *Death Can Wait.* He has always had a passion for telling suspenseful stories. Even at a young age, he was crafting horror stories to share with his family and friends. Evan Bond lives in Tampa, Florida with his wife, Melissa, their two boys, Desmond and Logan, and their cat and dog, Whiskey and Loki. When he's not writing, he can be found adventuring in the outdoors with his family and calling it "research" for his next novel.

Read more at https://www.evanbondauthor.com/.

www.ingramcontent.com/pod-product-compliance
Ingram Content Group UK Ltd.
Pitfield, Milton Keynes, MK11 3LW, UK
UKHW021936190726
13853UKWH00004B/1488